WELCOME TO THE EMPIRE

FIRST BOOK IN THE
REMOSIAN EMPIRE SAGA

MARK CURTO SR.

iUniverse, Inc.
Bloomington

Welcome to the Empire
First Book in the Remosian Empire Saga

iUniverse books may be ordered through booksellers or by contacting:

iUniverse
1663 Liberty Drive
Bloomington, IN 47403
www.iuniverse.com
1-800-Authors (1-800-288-4677)

ISBN: 978-1-4759-7970-1 (sc)
ISBN: 978-1-4759-7971-8 (ebk)

Library of Congress Control Number: 2013904059

Printed in the United States of America

iUniverse rev. date: 03/20/2013

CONTENTS

PROLOGUE

ALL WILL KNOW FEAR!

IT IS THE YEAR 3014. Battle rages above the Earth with an armada not seen in their lifetimes. Blasts of energy rain down upon the moon and Earth. The planetary shields hold, barely. Small silverfish tube looking ships maneuver the weapon platforms into better firing range. Larger flat vessels intercept the Earth's forces of tubular ships and missiles. A heavy ring of debris made of fallen ships and weapon platforms encircle the Earth. The battle rages.

The flagship of the armada looms high above overlooking the battle. The bridge bustles with activity as men in grey uniforms scurry about. Standing before the large windows of the bridge, staring out intently, is the leader of the armada. His white uniform almost glistens in the sun light. The gold crown on his head intermingles with his dark hair. His eyes give off a red hue. A slight crooked smile spreads across his face as he taps the ornate sword hanging on the right side of his belt. He is the first King of the Proprietorship.

"Admiral," the King barks without turning, "maneuver the weapon platforms into range of the moon. Since we cannot breach Earth's shields we will crush the moon and let the debris do it for us."

A short gray haired man stands at attention next to the King. "Sire, the moon was promised to the Eugenitors for payment of their alliance. Doing this will cut well into our profits and could reignite the conflict between us," the Admiral explains.

"I understand that Admiral but the energy and time we are wasting trying to breach those shields will soon exceed the profit. We can let them strip the northern Mars Colony instead."

"As you wish it, Sire," the Admiral backs away with a bow.

The King continues to stand at the giant windows of the bridge staring out with a broader crooked grin on his face. The large cannons start firing on the moon. The impacts of energy rip larger and larger chunks with a fog of dust and debris scattering throughout. The Earth's gravity takes hold. A steady stream of debris from the moon falls into the Earth's planetary shields. Brighter and brighter white flashes occur with each impact.

"King Marckolius, we have delivered the three religious leaders from the planet as requested. We demand you honor your word and stop the attack."

The King majestically turns and moves to stand in front of the uniformed officer from Earth in the blink of an eye. The King's ornate blood covered sword protrudes from the officer's back. Bright red drops hit the floor of the bridge forming a small puddle. The King's eyes, with a red hue and anger, stare at the three religious leaders' decorative dress. "You're a little late!" The King whispers into the officer's ear, loud enough for those around him to hear. With a sweeping motion, he pulls the sword from the now dead officer, wiping the blade clean with the officer's coat as the officer liquidates in front of everyone. Blood splatters up and down leaving a large puddle of his blood soaked cloths with no body found.

"You three once helped me become the King of the Proprietorship. Recently you dared to try and turn the members of the Proprietorship against me, a turn of conscious that has brought you here before me this day." The King motions with a hand and the guards thrust the three against the bridge windows overlooking the moon debris falling into the Earth's shields. The King grabs each one by their hair forcing them to watch. "You will observe the death of your precious Earth!"

"God will smite you and your evil spa . . ." One of the religious leaders words trail off as the King strikes his back, fracturing it. The man slumps forward, moaning in pain.

The King pulls one of the guards over, "Hold his Holiness up. He shouldn't miss this."

The flashes continue to brighten as the moon's debris hits the Earth's shields in ever-larger chunks. The now deformed moon moves faster toward the Earth. "Force their eyes open. I want them to see their handy work." Tears roll down their faces as they whisper prayers to themselves. "Your God isn't going to save you or them down there." King Marckolius gloats.

The deformed moon rushes into the Earth's shields causing the brightest flash seen yet. The flash is blinding. All of the ships in the armada lose their sensors and scanning capabilities. The flash lasts for a long time before dimming. The Earth is gone. No dust, debris, or any other remnant is left.

"Get those sensors back on line and find out the status of the armada," orders the Admiral.

The King stands speechless in front of the large windows of the bridge. He snaps back slowly and shakes his head in dismay. "One for the history books," he says to himself with a chuckle. He looks down upon the three men and motions to the guards to step back. "Kill them and then clean up the mess."

The guards pull out their guns and shoot. The King stares down at the dead bodies. "With the end of the Earth now begins my reign as King of all." A truly evil grin spreads across his face, "And, all will know fear!"

CHAPTER 1

FROM BIRTH TO
TARGET IN ONE DAY

I T IS THE EVE OF the Summer Solstice of the year 8014. The setting sun's reflection turns the first of two moons into a crimson full moon. The event heralded by cults and religious leaders alike is coming to fruition. The deadliest of all Destroyers is about to be born.

Within the palace, brightly lit hallways dim to almost darkness. Royal Guardsmen race to investigate. The assassins catch them from behind leaving their bodies left in pools of their own blood. The masked assassins silently move as their shadows follow behind. They spread out through the palace leaving dead guards in their wake.

The one man who has the most to lose, Duke Yoritus, feels that panic. The Duke, after much consulting with the Seers, confronts his brother, the King. He matches his quick pace through the ornate halls of the palace while surrounded by Royal Guardsmen.

"What is it Yori? I do not have time for fanatical rhetoric. Lady Marylyn is about to give birth and I want to be there to congratulate Captain Astanov."

The Duke steps in front of his brother stopping him. Beads of sweat glisten atop his baldhead. He looks his brother square in the eyes. "This is more than just our Captain of the Royal Guard having his son born."

The King steps back and looks at his disheveled brother. "You must have run from the other side of the palace. Why do you continue to listen to those harbingers of doom anyways?"

"The Seers know what they are talking about. They can read the vibrations of the future rippling through our time. Your son is going to born tonight and with him the beginning of the end of our power, our wealth, and our family!"

"Are you mad? My son is not to be born for two more weeks. We have been over this repeatedly. Now step aside!"

"I don't care what you think you know!" The Duke steps in front of his brother again, "The Seers have been right thus far and the Prophesy of the Gregorian Larch is about to come to fruition."

"When did you start to believe in God anyways?" The King sarcastically asks. "You despise all things religious, including my Queen."

"You married whom many would consider a witch!"

"I married the Priestess of the Holy Temple on Gregoria." The King's voice rises louder. "She is no witch!"

"When that second full moon rises and turns to blood he will be born, the reincarnation of the First King!" Duke Yoritus states as his eyes display a blood red hue. "You must understand this!"

"That is the belief of cults and fools."

Screeching sirens sound throughout the palace. The Duke hits the communicator on his dark brown leather gauntlet to hear the words, *"Assassins in the palace!"*

"We have to protect the Queen. Lock down the palace and get all available guards to the Medical Wing. Communication protocol zeta is now in effect," the King orders.

"The Duad Bantam is likely behind this. Our guards won't stand a chance against them."

"Then it's up to you to even the odds. Do what you do best Yori, kill!"

The Duke stares after the King as he walks briskly down the hall with his guards.

Captain Astonov greets the King as he arrives at the medical wing of the palace.

"You are late my friend," Captain Astonov chuckles. "My wife gave birth a while ago to a fine young boy."

They hug briefly, "I am so happy for you. In a couple of weeks, he will have a playmate. The sound of little feet will drive our wives crazy. What did you name him?"

"She named him Viktorlo, after her grandfather. I need to meet up with the guards and root out the assassins."

"Your place is here. Let Yori handle this. He believes it is the Duad Bantam." The King explains in almost a whisper.

"Then he is best to handle this. But we need to get the Queen out of the palace and possibly off-world."

"Agreed, our best bet is the gate since the landing pads will be the first place an assassin would lay in wait."

"We should have a straight shot to it. I will order the guards to shut down all of the hallways with the blast doors and stand guard inside the area. We will keep the path clear for the Queen and you."

The King pats Captain Astonov on the back, "I know you will old friend. We will get both our wives and your child to safety."

Captain Astonov motions over one of the guards and explains the plan to him. The guard bows to the King and leaves. They enter the recovery room. Lady Marylyn lies in the bed with her newborn son.

The Queen sits by her side. "You are late." The Queen says as the Kings bends down and hugs her.

"I love you too my dear." The King whispers in her ear. "Some official business came up."

"Yes, I heard the sirens."

"We will have to leave in a few minutes, just a precautionary measure."

Captain Astonov sits on the other side of the bed. The window in the room shows two blood moons now rising together over the skyline of the capital city. The large skyscrapers look small in comparison to the night sky's canopy framing the moons as they reflect the light giving the city a blood red hue.

"Would you look at that," Captain Astonov starts, "I don't think I have ever seen or heard of two blood moons rising at the same time."

"No one has." The clock in the room chimes midnight. The King's thoughts hearken back to his brother's words. He shakes his head and looks down at his wife. She is in visible distress.

"My water just broke." The Queen cries out. "Oh God, I'm in labor!"

The King summons the orderlies. They rush in with a hover chair and help the Queen into it. The King follows as she is whisked to the delivery room. Within the hour, the sound of a crying baby reverberates through the halls catching everyone's attention, including the assassins.

The two full blood moons rise to become one in the night sky, Duke Yoritus steps back from the window. His hands clench into fists. His dark brown eyes remain fixed on the blood moons. The echo of the baby's cry rattles throughout his mind.

A pale, brown robed man walks into the room and bows before the Duke.

"I know what you're about to say Seer."

"We heard the psychic cry of the newborn boy. The assassins are too late." The Seer says.

The Duke turns to the Seer, "Tell me how I am supposed to deal with this."

"Both the mother and child will escape through the gate and remain gone for a long time. You need to gain your brother's trust and help protect their escape."

"Why would I turn my back on the Duad Bantam? They answer to me."

"Patience and planning is key my Duke. Start with the head of the Syndicate, Lord Koronide. Replace him with the Intican Ossurate. There will be time in the future to manipulate the boy and remove the mother."

"But that could take years?"

"Years to help the boy grow with your influence to become what you help mold him into. Think of the treasure and power you will gain. You will need it to build your armada."

"I told you before, the size of the armada required to destroy Gregoria is beyond the amount of profit I would gain. Even if I took out their allies first it would be years in the making. Years . . ." Duke Yoritus finishes as he grabs the robes of the Seer and peers into his yellowish white eyes.

"As we discussed, this is the way to get this done; slow and steady, without notice. Patience my Duke, patience, after all the Asmores have waited this long. They can wait years longer."

The Royal Guardsmen speed through the halls of the palace, clearing the path to the gate. The Queen and her child, Lady Marylyn and her child, the King, and Captain Astonov follow. Screams of pain and terror echo from behind them, in between the sounds of weapons' fire as the palace guards confront the assassins.

They enter the largest open-air room in the palace. In the center circle stand twelve tall white stone obelisks. The outer circle contains numerous smaller ones.

"Come on Marylyn," The Queen motions. "We will take our children to Gregoria for now and let the men take care of the problem."

"I will contact you once we have secured the palace and the grounds." The Kings hugs the Queen and his newborn son. "By the way, what are we naming him?"

"His name is Marckolius Taranus Anglicus."

"You named him after the First King?"

"I named him after much prayer and meditation. I named him what God wanted me to name him. Moreover, do not worry about the cults and fools out there. There is no such thing as reincarnation."

"You always know what I am thinking."

"Being psychic has its benefits my love."

Weapons fire echoes from the outside hall beyond the sealed doors to the gate room. "You must go. Do the thing you do and get out of here."

"I love you." The Queen turns toward the gate. She hands her son to Lady Marylyn who now holds both boys. She stretches out her arms as they move into the center of the obelisks. The strain shows on her face as she physically accesses the gate.

The gate comes to life with a glow from ancient runes on the obelisks. The King and Captain Astonov back away and watch as the energy envelops the Queen, Lady Marylyn and their sons. The clouds above the palace swirl. Loud cracks of thunder and lightning occur. With a loud crack of thunder heard by everyone inside the surrounding halls of the gate room, a large white column of energy shoots up from the center of the circle of obelisks and into the swirling sky above. They are gone. The swirling clouds rapidly dissipate.

The door to the gate room opens to reveal Duke Yoritus standing in the hallway with the blood soaked clothes of two assassins. Bodies of the guards, most of them dead, line the hallway.

"Sorry I took so long. Was that the gate I heard? I thought you would go to the landing pads."

"Yori, you have this knack for showing up at the oddest of times." The King says.

"Yes, well I did contact the outside regiment. They are combing the other side of the palace. I believe that the Duad Bantam has already escaped."

"Did you kill the shadow demon attached to each one of the assassins?" Captain Astonov asks as he examines the bloody cloths.

"I am no priest. They are dead. Now, if you will excuse me I am needed elsewhere."

After the Duke leaves, the King stands by the outer circle of obelisks and looks up at the clear skies.

"You know my old friend, our sons have a destiny."

Captain Astonov joins the King and looks up at the skies. "I agree, they will be great and they will do great things."

"That is if they survive childhood."

CHAPTER 2

ONE DAY . . .

'*WAKE UP!*'
       Staring out from what seems like a padded table in a dark room, fear grips Prince Marckolius. He cannot move. Pain shoots through his skull like lightning through a tree.

'WAKE UP!'

"He's awake." A familiar voice exclaims, "Shhhhhh, it's alright," He hears as his Aunt Marianus starts to unstrap him from the table. Her long brown robes keep getting in the way as she works on the straps. "You are lucky he woke up at all from this. No one this young should have this done to them."

"You know we had to do this or he would turn out like the rest of them!" His mother barks back as loud clanking noises and a bang echo through the room. "I'm here my brave young man." She says in a more calming tone as she appears before him. "You did very well."

"My head hurts." Marckolius hears himself cry out. "It hurts really bad mommy!"

'You have got to WAKE UP!'

"There, there, you are alright. Marianus, please get him something for the pain."

"Helena, do you think it worked?" His aunt injects him with a dark blue fluid.

A deep male voice from the far side of the room answers, "His vitals are fine High Priestess. But there is an odd side effect."

"Later Kismet!" His mother kisses him on the forehead, "Just rest . . . ."

'I said, WAKE UP!'

Prince Marckolius springs up in his bed covered in sweat. His night robes, pillow, and sheets are soaked through. His dark hair matted to his head. Beads of sweat pour down his dark tanned face.

"I'm up!" He barks out still recovering from his nightmare, "Lights."

The lights in his large bedroom come up causing the darkish figure by his bed to disappear rapidly.

"I saw you this time. Waking me up like this. What is your reason this time? It is only one in the morning. Don't you have souls to reap or something?"

'Your mother needs you.' The whispering voice echoes through his mind.

"My mother?"

His attention turns to voices outside in the hallway. Prince Marckolius bolts out of bed and runs over to the door. He can barely make out his mother and father arguing about something.

"You can't go just because she says she has some information for you." He hears his father say.

"I have to go. She was my responsibility. I'll be back in an hour or less." His mother answers. "Now, quiet before you wake our son."

The voices trail off down the hallway.

"What were they arguing about this time? Not my father's mistress or step brothers I hope."

The palace rattles just like when a small quake occurs. Thunder echoes through the halls as lightening arches through the skies above the palace.

"The gate just activated."

'Follow her.'

"Funny!"

"FOLLOW HER!"

"Fine, let me get dressed first." A perturbed Prince answers. "Why do I have to follow my mother through the gate? She's gone off plenty of times alone."

'Danger!'

Prince Marckolius slowly opens his bedroom door and moves as quietly as possible through the halls of the palace. He creeps up to the gate room and peers in. No one is there. He moves quickly to the center circle of white stone obelisks and outstretches his hands. In his mind, he sees a central orb of green pulsating energy. He reaches out and takes it in his hands. He sees the greenish string going off to another far endpoint.

"That's the path my mother took. That is the path I choose."

The ancient runes on the white obelisks glow with a white vibrant energy. The white energy surrounds the Prince as the skies above begin to swirl. Lightning ignites in the skies above. The energy grows until a loud crack of thunder echoes through the halls of the palace and forms a column of white energy into the center of the swirling clouds. The Prince is gone.

The skies above swirl. Lightning and thunder erupt from the clouds. From their center emerges a burst of white energy that shoots down to the white stone obelisks below. The white energy dissipates to show the Prince an unknown dark dilapidated place. He moves through a nearby doorway clutching a sword holstered to the right side of his belt. He hears the sounds of fighting ahead. Screams and pain come rushing to him.

'Hurry!'

"The gate just activated a second time. Go and see who comes." A growling voice echoes through the large dark cavernous room.

In the dark, the Prince makes out the brown and maroon auras of those coming to the doorway. He slips into the room and allows them to approach. As they do, almost like images in sand were being blown away from them, their faces and bodies change from those of vampires with sunken pale faces to what they once were, human. In the distance behind them, two other vampires are dragging his mother away.

The vampires notice the change and stop. The Prince pulls his sword and attacks all four. The vampires see the bright red hue from the Prince's eyes, just before they die. All that is left is the blood soaked clothing they wore. The Prince sprints as fast as he can picking up his mother's sword as he rushes towards her. The vampires dragging his mother away hear the wet footsteps and stop.

"Get your filthy hands off my mother!"

The leaping Prince slashes into their backs at the same time as their images quickly dissipate like blowing sand. Both disappear with an awful splattering sound as blood hits the floor and ceiling. His mother's legs hit the floor with a thud. The strong smell of iron permeates the air. Off in the distance two yellow eyes stare at the

Prince. Marckolius sees the auras of more vampires coming toward him in the dark. A separate slender figure runs from a far entrance to the room. The Prince stands with both swords in his hands, pulsing red hue eyes, and gritting teeth.

"Stop!" A raspy female voice yells out. "Stop this right now!" The figure running from the other entrance stops in front of the approaching vampires. She is also a vampire with a slightly lighter aura than the others have, "Osserate, tell them to stop, you want more of your elites to die?"

"You heard her. Any ways, the boy is not on the contract. Our work is done. She will be dead by morning." the same growling echoing voice from before states.

The female vampire approaches cautiously. Her skin is a pale scaly version of the others. She stares at the Prince with light green eyes as her face changes. The vampire image falls away to show her natural sparkling skin and beautiful face.

"I am not going to hurt you or your mother." She says softly. "Please, I need to check her injuries."

The Prince puts his swords down only slightly allowing her to kneel beside his mother. "Who are you?"

"My name is Anna. Your mother and I have known each other for many years." She pulls away some of his mother's bloody garments.

"You were once a Eugenitor?"

"Your mother is alive but unconscious." She holds up his mother's right arm. "You see these two puncture holes? She has been bitten. That means the blood born disease that causes vampirism is spreading through her system. You need to get her home quickly."

"Yes, yes." The Prince feels he can trust her and holsters both swords.

"I will help you get her to the gate."

Each one takes an arm and starts to pull her to the gate room.

"Let me explain something. You must promise me not return here until you are seventeen. If you do, Osserate will kill you. He has a demon stone that gives him added strength, agility, and speed. You would not be a match for him at this time. How old are you right now?"

"I will be ten soon," The Prince's voice strains.

They pull his mother to the center of the white obelisks. The Prince notices how tall Anna is.

"Thank you for your help."

"So polite too, everything your mother said you are. You understand what you must do when you return to Propri?"

"I have to perform the purification rite to stop the spreading of the disease." The Prince answers as he outstretches his arms.

"She is badly injured and may not survive. Remember; do not return here until you are seventeen. Train hard and learn everything you can from your aunt." Anna backs out of the gate room.

The Prince nods as the runes on the obelisks start to glow a vibrant white. The clouds swirl, lightning, and thunder erupt. The white energy encompasses both the Prince and his mother. In an instant, the white column forms from the ground to the swirling clouds above. The Prince and his mother are gone.

Guards patrol the gate room on Propri. The guards' attention focuses on the sound of lightning and thunder from above. They back away and sound the alarm as the runes on the white obelisks begin to glow. A white energy column shoots down into the center circle of the obelisks as the King and Captain of the Guard enter. The clap of thunder that echoes through the palace is almost deafening. The Prince appears, standing next to his mother's unconscious body.

The guards rush to them.

"Get her to the medical wing. I need something from the chapel." The Prince runs towards the door.

His father stops him, "You need to be checked for injuries. You have blood all over your clothes."

"Don't worry, none of it is mine. I need to get the holy chrism from the chapel. She was bitten by a vampire before I got there." The Prince breaks free and races down the hall.

He runs into the chapel located near the personal bedrooms. The strong smell of roses hits him as he pulls out the small wooden chest from behind a set of red and white satin curtains. He pulls out his mother's sword and places the tip into the lock. With a bluish spark, the lock clicks and the chest opens with a swooshing noise. He grabs two vials of slightly glowing clear thick oil.

He runs through the halls toward the medical wing of the palace. A boy bumps into him as he turns a corner.

"Viktorlo?" Prince Marckolius checks the vials.

"Marckolius, I heard there was some sort of emergency." Viktorlo stands brushing himself off.

"I need to get to the medical wing." The Prince sprints off again with Viktorlo running behind him.

"There's blood all over your clothes. You've been in a fight?"

"Vampires!"

"Where? How many?"

"I will have to tell you later." The Prince speeds ahead.

He bursts into the room to see is father standing beside his mother discussing something with the doctor.

"Son, please come over here. I need to talk with you." The King somberly motions to Marckolius.

The Prince moves past the doctor to his mother and grabs her right arm. He rips the bandage off the puncture wounds.

"Son, what are you doing?" The King grabs his sons shoulder and spins him around.

"She was bitten by a vampire. I need to purify the wound area before the disease has a chance to take hold."

"Slow down. Your mother is in a coma from her injuries and blood loss. She's dying." The King sobs.

"This will kill the disease before it turns her into one of those things." The Prince tries to explain.

Prince Marckolius turns back. He pulls the plug from one of the vials, and rubs the oil into the puncture wounds. He starts muttering the purification prayers as if he has known them all his life. He opens the second vial and places drops on his mother's closed eyes, nose, and mouth. He rubs the rest of the vial into the puncture wounds. He holds his mother's hand as she convulses. White vapors rise from her mouth and the puncture wounds on her right arm.

The Prince feels a change in her. Her purification is complete but her injuries are too much to overcome.

He hears the faint voice of his mother in his head, '*I am so sorry Marckolius, but I have to go.*'

"No mother!" Marckolius cries out. "You can't go."

'*I am dying my son. You saved me. You really did. I am so proud of you.*' Her voice trails off.

Prince Marckolius bows his head. Tears stream from his eyes. The monitors all go flat.

'*She's gone.*' The other male voice softly whispers to the Prince.

"I know."

His father bends over and hugs them both. After a long while, the King pulls Marckolius away from his mother.

"They need to prepare her for burial." The Kings says as he wipes the tears from his eyes.

They walk out into the outer hall area where there is a very somber gathering of many palace residents. The Duke approaches the King and Prince and hugs them both. He kneels down and looks the Prince in the eyes as he places his hands on his shoulders.

"You were very brave. Viktorlo says you fought vampires?"

Flashes and images stream into Marckolius' mind, an image stronger than the others becomes clear. He closes his eyes and sees a contract on a table. A large hairy man sits with a very toothy smile. The man's yellow eyes widen as someone signs the contract.

"*Osserate, make sure she dies bloody*" he hears his uncle command.

"*You are the customer my Duke.*" *A jovial Osserate reaches out and shakes Duke Yoritus' hand.*

The Prince's crystal blue eyes open with a bright red hue. He stares straight into his uncle's eyes.

"YOU DID THIS! You betrayed us!" He yells as he pushes his uncle away.

"Marckolius," his father attempts to grab his son. "What is the meaning of this?"

The Prince faces his father. He points at his uncle. "He did this. He signed the contract with Osserate. I saw it."

"My brother, I know he is distraught but you must calm him. You need to explain to the young Prince that you cannot make such outlandish accusations without physical proof."

The King grabs his son and pulls him close.

"I saw him sign the contract. The images came from him." The weeping Prince mutters.

"Shhhh, it will be alright. You may have misinterpreted something. This has happened before."

"My brother," Duke Yoritus begins, "We will need to discuss the burial preparations. It is best if the young Prince retires to his quarters. It has been a long day for him."

The King nods. "Marckolius, return to your quarters and get cleaned up. Rest for a while. We will have something for you to eat brought up to you. It will be a long week ahead for all of us. Now go."

Prince Marckolius nods. On the way into the hallway, he gives his uncle an enraged glance. "One day uncle I will bring you to justice," he mutters under his voice. Once outside of the room, memories flash through his mind; his uncle training him in swordsmanship, hand to hand combat, and tactics. Tears roll down his face. He grits his teeth and clenches his fists. "My mother warned me of them. They only care about profit and would sacrifice the ones they love for it." The Prince wipes his tears away.

'Keep walking.'

"One day . . . ." Prince Marckolius mutters.

CHAPTER 3

THERE'S MORE OUT THERE.
INTERESTED?

T HE PRINCE AND HIS FRIEND Viktorlo are strapped into the military personnel section of a transport. Soldiers in white heavy camouflage fatigues surround them. The soldiers all wear white gloves and carry white painted weapons. The vibrations from the engines indicate that they are in Interdimensional Space.

"So your father thought it was a good idea for us to go along to see the changing of the guard at one of your family's mining facilities?" Viktorlo asks while leaning in close to Prince Marckolius.

"My father ordered me to go along because it would be educational. Your father volunteered you to accompany me because I needed a bodyguard. Think of it as an early birthday present. We are almost fourteen." The Prince explains.

"You do know that we don't have a very good track record when it comes to our travels."

"Yeah, I know."

"Assassination attempts, sabotage, and plenty of other issues keep happening to us. We are the unluckiest set of misfits in the Proprietorship."

"Sarcasm?"

"Truth!"

"You two keep it down. Some of us are trying to nap," a soldier says.

Viktorlo leans in and whispers to Prince Marckolius, "I've got a bad feeling about this."

"Your bad feelings often turn into us intervening. Quit with the bad mojo."

"Look and see if the hairs on the back of my neck are standing up."

"No."

"It feels like the hairs on the back of my neck are standing up. You know what that means."

'Danger!'

Prince Marckolius smacks Viktorlo in the chest. "Stop it. We should be coming out of Interdimensional Space any time now. Be ready just in case you are right."

The tone and vibration of the engines change. With a flash of bluish light, the transport exits Interdimensional Space.

'Be at the ready.'

"The Captain should be contacting the tower anytime now." Viktorlo leans in.

"You still have that bad feeling?"

"Yep, worse than ever."

"Why are you two with us real men anyways?" A soldier sitting next to Prince Marckolius asks.

"We aren't children if that's what you are implying." Viktorlo snaps back.

"Then why do we feel like baby sitters?" Another soldier jokes. Many of the others laugh loudly.

"It's fine for you to laugh and chuckle at our expense. Just be ready to go." A slight irritation in the Prince's voice eggs the soldiers on as the Prince scans the group. 'These guys are newly paid help. They don't really know who we are," The Prince thinks to himself. "You all know I am the Prince, right?"

The soldiers' blank stares show embarrassment. "Sorry my Prince but if you think you are about to visit a winter wonderland, then the only thing you got right is the winter part." Another soldier jokes.

The soldier across from Viktorlo and the Prince leans forward with a smile, "If the stories are true then you both should have no trouble at all."

Prince Marckolius chuckles. The Intercom screeches to life, "This is the Captain. We have been unable to raise the tower. We will attempt to approach from the south. Everyone remain strapped in and ready."

"Nice, here we are stuck with a bunch of morons." Viktorlo leans in to the Prince. "You know we are the ones that are going to have to save their sorry asses!"

"Sarcasm again?"

"Truth, it always seems that way."

"Oh yeah, by the way Viktorlo, these guys are not our normal detail. They had no idea who we are before I told them. They thought we were teens hitching a ride home."

Viktorlo shakes his head, "Figures, your uncle's doing no doubt."

Everyone feels the banking of the transport. The sounds of laser blasts and near explosions echo through the hull.

"Those are cannon shots impacting on the shields." An anxious soldier exclaims.

"We are taking fire from the tower. Prepare for emergency landing." The intercom belches just as a harsh blast echoes through the transport.

'Move!'

The blast doors to the cockpit bulge but do not give. The lights go out in the banking transport. Prince Marckolius takes the straps off and pulls a blue crystal from his pocket. He works his way a couple of meters to the blast door controls leading to the cockpit. He pulls the control panel cover off and places the crystal into a hidden socket. The doors partially open. The soldiers strain to open the doors more as snow pelts them. Marckolius places the crystal back into his pants pocket without notice.

'Pull up the nose.'

Marckolius yells over the howling winds, "There's just enough room to slip in. We have to pull the transport's nose up."

Marckolius and Viktorlo move the charred bodies of the Captain and Co-captain out of the way and sit in the burnt seats. The control panels are partially lit but sparking. Both pull back as hard as they can on the joysticks to raise the nose of the transport. The ship slowly responds with the loud sounds of groans and metal cracking. The nose lifts up as the snow covered ground approaches.

"Brace your legs against the dashboard's metal frame." Viktorlo yells.

Both lift their legs up wedging their heavy winter boots into the steel frame of the cockpit dash while still pulling back on the joysticks. The back half of the transport hits the snow first. The sliding continues as the front hits the snow. The transport goes for some distance before stopping. Both Viktorlo and Prince Marckolius are covered head to toe with snow. They unstick themselves and crawl back through the blast doors.

"Are all of you alright? Sound off!" Viktorlo commands as the wind howls through the open cockpit windows.

Twelve men sound off with no injuries to report.

Prince Marckolius looks to the two closest men. "You two, go to the storage area and pull out the scopes, food, and heated water." Both bow and move to the back of the transport. "The rest of you, unstrap yourselves and lineup to receive your rations. We are not going to wait for whomever to come and finish us off. We are going to them."

"Put your com units in place and test them one at a time." Viktorlo commands.

Each of the soldier's com links work fine. The soldiers in the storage area pass up the winter packs. Everyone takes one, including Viktorlo and Prince Marckolius.

"Get out there and secure the area. Take a distance reading to the tower." Viktorlo commands.

"Tower sir?" A soldier asks.

"Each mining facility has an armed control tower with all of the communications and rotary cannon for protection. That tower is at the center of the facility surrounded by a perimeter wall. Now, get out there and secure the area," the Prince orders.

The soldiers stream out of the ship in zigzag formations, covering and securing the perimeter outside of the ship. They measure the distance to the tower.

"The tower and mining facility is just over two kilometers north from our position, Sir. No one is coming."

"Whoever shot us down must not be able to spare anyone to come out here." Viktorlo ponders.

"Or they think we died in the crash. Even with no explosion it would have been difficult to survive if we hadn't pulled the nose up." The Prince looks at the crumpled nose of the transport. "Let's move out. We've had our fill of this winter wonderland."

After a long walk in the driving snow, they reach the outside area of the mining facility. Two guards secure the way into the facility. Their black coats and weather gear make them stand out against the backdrop of the falling snow.

"We need to take them down without notice." Prince Marckolius says to Viktorlo.

"Those are heated suits." Viktorlo notices as he looks through one of the scopes. "Who would have heated suits?"

"Vampires, they hate the cold more than we do. They freeze up like lizards in the cold." Prince Marckolius explains. "You take the one on the left. I will take the one on the right." Both pull out their swords. The Prince turns to the soldiers. "Be ready but stay here. Once those two are dead we will motion for you to come."

"But Sir, shouldn't we be doing this?"

"No!" Viktorlo answers quickly. "You'd be dead on approach. Leave it to us."

The soldiers watch. In the blink of an eye, the guards' helmets roll off into the deep snow. Their blood-filled suits fall to the ground turning the snow red. A red hue from both the Prince's and Viktorlo's eyes is clearly visible. They motion for the soldiers to come.

They maneuver through the landing bay and work areas. A large transport helps give them cover. A conveyer belt rolls square cubes of ore into the transport with loud continuous clanking noise.

"Take a look at the markings on the transport," Viktorlo points to a symbol on the ship that has an eye with a capital 'S' in the eyeball, "The Syndicate!"

The Prince motions to the soldiers to move ahead. They give the all clear and move into the building. Inside they continue to move slowly. The panels for monitoring the mines are dead. They hear a fight going on farther ahead. Moving slowly they see two vampires keeping their distance from a tall teen boy with long blond locks and dirty leather pants and shirt. He is wielding a large axe.

They watch as the teen moves forward enough to cause one of the vampire's image to fall away like blowing sand. He swings the axe into the vampire, bursting him in an instant. Blood splatters as the other vampire turns away. His image falls away as he runs into Viktorlo's sword. The vampire bursts and splatters like the other.

The teen picks up his axe and approaches the Prince and Viktorlo. He sees the red hue in their eyes just as they see the red hue in his.

"I'm Brianto, son of the second in command of this facility."

"This is Viktorlo and I'm Prince Marckolius."

"My Prince," Brianto bows. "I had heard you were coming before all this happened."

"Where are the families and the soldiers that were supposed to guard the facility?"

"The families are back that way where I was preventing those things from entering. The magistrate went up to the tower office with some big hairy wolf man animal thing. The guards are all dead, including my father, as they tried to fight off those things we just killed."

"I'm sorry to hear that." Prince Marckolius starts. "Half of you soldiers go with him and guard the families. The rest go with Viktorlo and stop the loading of the ore cubes. I will take care of the magistrate and the Intican with him."

Viktorlo grabs the Prince's shoulder with a look of concern. "You've never fought one of them before."

"Remember, my aunt's teachings and training has been very thorough. It's time to put all that training to the test." The Prince turns to Brianto, "Which way to the tower?"

"The elevator went down after the defense system and mining systems shorted out. The stairs are on the other side that way," Brianto points.

"All of you go. I have business to conduct."

Brianto looks at Viktorlo inquisitively.

"He's being sarcastic. All of you go!" Viktorlo motions to the soldiers.

They split off to their various assignments. The Prince sheds his heavy white camouflage coat and gloves. The sprint up the tower steps does not faze him as it would a normal human or well-trained soldier. He reaches the top after some minutes to find a small landing and a large office door. Two vampires stand guard. They rush towards him without realizing the change occurs. Blood splatters making the stairs and landing slick.

The Prince listens beside the thick door. He hears a conversation but cannot make out the words. He pulls the cover off the door lock built within the wall. He places the blue crystal from his pocket into the hidden slot. The lock clicks open. He places the crystal back into his pants pocket and pushes the door open with his sword. He moves into the large round office and off to side very quickly. Large windows look out all around to the wintery landscape.

The Prince sees the magistrate sitting in his chair behind the large desk and console area. The large hairy Intican next to him stares at the Prince with yellowish eyes, gripping the magistrate's neck. The Prince meets his stare.

"I see they send a boy to do a man's job." The Intican starts. "You move closer and the magistrate dies. I will snap his neck like a small twig."

"Please, I had no choice." The magistrate pleads.

Even from this distance, the Prince is able to sense the collusion between the magistrate and the Intican. The Intican is much harder to read.

"My dear magistrate," The Prince begins, "You are dead either way."

"Then there is no point in trying to negotiate with you?" The Intican moves his hands into position on the magistrate's head.

"Why is the Syndicate stealing ore cubes from us?"

'Careful!'

"We were contracted to pick up the ore cubes for delivery. Did you want a fee reimbursement, payment for the dock fees, or additional surcharge payment?"

'Careful!'

The Prince continues trying to scan the Intican. An accidental brain spike causes a sharp pain to the Intican.

"You're in my head!" He exclaims as he snaps the neck of the magistrate. He spins around smashing through the large window behind him.

"Ah crap!" The Prince jumps over the desk, past the dead magistrate, and out the window behind the Intican into a diving position to speed his descent.

The snow and winds calm as they drop to the ship dock area below. The Intican lands on the top of a large forklift leaving little space beneath. The Intican lets out a loud yelp as the Prince lands on his back. The Prince slices into the Intican's side with his sword.

"Get off me you punk!" The Intican throws the Prince across the ship dock area.

The Intican jumps off the forklift in the direction of Prince Marckolius. The Prince slides to a stop in a three-point stance with his blood tipped sword at the ready.

"You will pay for that boy!" The Intican angrily sprints toward the Prince.

The Prince dodges and parries each blow. He scans the Intican for information while fighting the creature to a stalemate.

The Prince pulls back some, "Your name is Francis?"

"It's Francisco," The Intican snaps back jumping at the Prince.

Both Viktorlo and Brianto arrive at the ship dock area. Brianto lifts his axe to attack.

Viktorlo puts his arm up blocking him from moving. "Watch for it."

"Watch for what?"

The Prince keeps parrying and parrying until the Intican pauses for a brief second.

"That!"

The Intican's head rolls off his body with a 'swoosh' of the Prince's sword. The body falls forward at his feet. The Prince looks over to see Viktorlo and Brianto standing by the facility entrance with a few of the guards. As the Prince walks over to them, the red hue in his eyes clears away.

"Let's go in and warm up, shall we?"

"So, what did you learn from the Intican?" Viktorlo asks.

"His name was Francisco and no, he had nothing to do with my mother's death."

"Was he a rogue or still working as part of the Syndicate?"

"I thought it was best to end the fight. I was getting cold."

"You mean to tell me that you were able to read his mind?" Astonishment spreads across Brianto's face.

"It takes a lot of effort; otherwise, he would have been dead up in the tower."

"So the training worked?"

"What, what training?"

"Yes, my aunt's training works. She's a Demon Hunter. And you could go through the training too." The Prince answers turning to Brianto. "You and your mother should come to the palace."

"I don't understand."

"We train and have direct tutoring, loads of fun." Viktorlo smiles broadly.

Prince Marckolius turns to face them. "Brianto, it's dangerous. We end up in situations that push us continuously. We train to survive these types of events with training provided by our trainers in the palace and well outside of the palace too. We are learning and training for our future."

"You are going to scare him." Viktorlo interjects.

"You mean we get to fight and kill things?"

"You sound excited." Viktorlo looks oddly at Brianto.

"Those things were vampires and that hairy thing was an Intican." Prince Marckolius explains. "There's more out there. Interested?"

CHAPTER 4

GOD IS WATCHING

THE CLOUDS SWIRL ABOVE THE Great Temple on Gregoria. Lightning flashes. Loud cracks of thunder cause the skyscrapers to vibrate. A column of white energy departs the swirling clouds and enters the temple through a large circular opening in its golden oval dome. Standing in the center to the left is Brianto. He holds a sword in one hand and a battle-axe in the other. In the center of the three is Viktorlo with his hands outstretched. Prince Marckolius stands to the right of them with his sword in his right hand.

"Beautiful entrance my nephew." A voice from the darkness calls out. "At the ready I see, prepared for anything just as you three were taught."

"Put your weapons away. My aunt is the only one in the Great Temple, besides the guards." Prince Marckolius points down the long center white and gold marble path.

His Aunt Marianus walks forward into the candle light, adjusting her brown robes. "You three are very punctual." She hugs her nephew. "You let Viktorlo drive I see."

"He must practice."

She hugs Viktorlo and then Brianto. "How old are you boys now, seventeen I believe?"

"Yes we are. We just celebrated our birthdays." Viktorlo answers proudly.

"Well, mine was a couple months ago but we celebrated them together on Cantara." Brianto proclaims.

"We need to get a move on or you'll be late. The Council will not like that." Sister Marianus hands each of them a thick brown robe and motions for them to walk with her. "Adjust your robes. They are easily offended by decorative dress."

"Other than their own?" Viktorlo and the Prince chuckle at the rhetorical question.

They leave through the large ornate wooden doors in the very back of the Great Temple and walk together into a large well-lit hallway.

"Well now, you three went to Cantara to celebrate your birthdays and the entering of manhood?" She asks as they walk. "You three wouldn't have had anything to do with the untimely demolition of an entire city block?"

"I think she already knows the answer."

"Don't push her Brianto. Remember who we are walking with," Viktorlo chuckles.

"Two of the Duad Bantam decided to crash our party." Prince Marckolius explains. "We tracked them to their hideout, in an old abandoned hotel. We tried to subdue them but ended up killing them instead. I think we need more practice."

"Of course you need more practice!" She exclaims. "You are supposed to sift the shadow demon from their body and eradicate it. You are not supposed to kill the host. You three have got to learn control."

"But we need more practice." Brianto chimes in. "Practicing on dummies or bio-drones just doesn't cut it."

"I was thinking about that. How about if I contract the Syndicate to capture us a pair so we can practice on the real thing?"

Sister Marianus stops, spins around, and stares her nephew square in his crystal blue eyes. "You wouldn't! Such a contract would be considered heinous. You were raised better than that!"

"Would it be considered wrong to hire vampires to capture and subdue demons for the explicit intention of bettering our skills? I do not see how this would be heinous. You said it yourself that we need to practice."

"You have no regard for the host. Remember you three, the host may not be innocent but the host is still a human and may have been forced into the arrangement." Sister Marianus turns and starts walking down the long hallway again.

"Why did the Council ask for us to come?" Viktorlo asks.

"Is it the fuel crisis or is it the fact that we are going to the fortress on Desespero, the seat of the Syndicate?" Prince Marckolius catches up to his aunt.

"Both!" Sister Marianus barks. "They have a proposal for you and a request. They know that you are to meet with the Syndicate and learn how to negotiate high-level contracts with your father's chief contract negotiator. And, you already know that Osserate is the head of the Syndicate."

"So?" Viktorlo blurts out. "Are they expecting us to renegotiate your contract with the Syndicate for the Proprietorship's fuel waste?"

"Clever boy, yes they are. I suggest you do not go there at all. You will be needlessly putting yourselves in harm's way."

"Oh, and the two maybe three assassination attempts, being taken hostage, and being caught in a firefight between two different races isn't being in harm's way? Just getting up out of bed puts us in harm's way!"

"Brianto has a funny way of saying we are screwed no matter what," interrupts Viktorlo. "But there is some strategic value in going."

"You must understand, we didn't ask for this life. It's time I return to Desespero to set things right by ending Osserate."

"You mean to kill him, don't you? Are you ready for such a task?" She lets out a deep sigh. "The choice is yours. I will wait here while you three enter the Council Chambers."

"He was the principle in the death of my mother, your sister. That doesn't mean anything to you?" Anger fills the Prince's words.

"And what about them?" Sister Marianus points at Viktorlo and Brianto.

"What about us?" Both Viktorlo and Brianto answer at the same time.

"Did he give you a choice?"

"Sister Marianus, we do this not just out of obligation to the Prince but out of an internal drive that you could not understand." Viktorlo tries to explain.

"Why, to feed your blood lust?"

"Because of what we are! There is a fire, a thirst, a hunger that drives through our veins." Prince Marckolius answers. "We've learned control through you and others but it's why Destroyers are feared throughout time. If a Destroyer gives in to these urges then evil, death, destruction, hell, and mayhem will follow wherever he goes. The older you get the stronger it grow."

"You make yourselves sound like vampires."

"In a way, we have more in common with vampires than we do normal run of the mill humans. Our drive is not out of necessity of life unlike theirs."

After a short pause, Sister Marianus points forward, "You three really need to go." They walk forward. The Prince looks back to see his aunt scowling back at him.

They enter a large golden marble room. Two guards stand in front of a pair of brilliantly colored elevator doors at the far end. A dark robed priest stands between them holding a digital pad.

"They are expecting you Brother Marckolius. Your two friends have to wait here."

"Doubt it. They will be coming down with me and no words about it."

"They won't like it!"

"They will get over it."

The three enter the elevator and begin their decent. Almost a minute passes before the elevator stops and the doors open to a large onyx walled room. Eight white robed men sit behind a semi-circle cream marble table. Sitting in the center behind the table is a white and red robed man of much older stature, the Gregorian Larch.

As Prince Marckolius, Viktorlo, and Brianto exit the elevator, the white robed man to the right of the Gregorian Larch stands, "Your friends can stand over to the right." He points.

Prince Marckolius motions to Viktorlo and Brianto. They walk over to the darkest part of the room. The Prince walks forward until he stands in the center before the table of council members. He looks his grandfather in the eyes, the Gregorian Larch. The standing council member sits as the lights dim. The brightest light in the room shines on Prince Marckolius.

"We asked you to come here this day to give you a mission of utmost importance." One of the council members begins. "We request, that since you are already going to Desespero, that you assist us in convincing the Syndicate to renew our contract with them and begin shipping us the fuel we need."

Prince Marckolius cracks a slight smile. "I've heard you let the fuel shortages become so bad that most merchants have doubled their prices. How could you not have done something about this on your own?"

"As part of this mission you and your friends will be given complete dispensation up to and including killing Osserate, if it is required." The council member ignores the Prince's question. "Brother Marckolius, do you accept the mission?"

'Ask the question.' Prince Marckolius hears in his mind.

"What of my friends' official ranking within the Church?" The council members return a puzzling look. "Simply put, they have completed the training. Why not give them and others official ranks as Warriors? Why not allow those who hear the calling to become priests?"

"They are not Gregorians." One of the council members answers.

"So? I'm only half Gregorian. This council discriminates."

"We do not need a lecture from the likes of you. Do you or do you not accept the mission?" The lead council member asks.

"I am inclined to say no for as long as this council continues to discriminate."

"Guards!" The council member to the right of the Gregorian Larch stands. "Remove them from this holy chamber."

Before anyone could blink Viktorlo and Brianto move, placing a hand on each of the guards, freezing them both in mid-step.

"You should be thanking Viktorlo and Brianto for saving the lives of your two guards. If they had continued forward both would have died leaving a bloody pool of soaked clothing behind."

Speechless, the council member sits down. Prince Marckolius steps forward with his eyes closed. He moves his head as if to look at each council member. Some nervousness spreads among the Council.

"Now then, each of you will answer this question. DOES GOD DISCRIMINATE AGAINST THOSE WHO ARE WORTHY?" Each of the council members answers no, except for one. "Councilman Tremono," Prince Marckolius steps forward and places both his hands on the table before him. He opens his eyes to show the bright red hue. The hue seems to pulse and light up the face of the council member. "DOES GOD DISCRIMINATE AGAINST THOSE WHO ARE WORTHY?" The question pierces Tremono's mind like a dagger.

"Why is it so hard for you to answer a simple question?" The Gregorian Larch softly chimes in. "You know the answer, why do this?"

The council member's eyes remain locked with Prince's, "The answer is NO! Alright, the answer is no."

Prince Marckolius releases him as the council member falls back in his chair. He looks at the other council members, "I apologize for asking the question so forcibly. Your ranks are dwindling. Your influence flounders daily. Your oppressiveness upon this population and others brings more and more disdain. You are about to lose what allies you have left, all because this Council continues to govern with a clenched fist. Does everything have to have some type of religious metaphor or connotation? Does everyone have to be at least partly Gregorian by blood? You admit that God does not discriminate but you do!"

The Gregorian Larch explains, "These laws were passed to help protect our society. The people must be guided to truth. They will stumble if left to their own conventions."

"You have gone so far as to prohibit foreigners from entering our churches and temples, our society, the priesthood, to become more than what they are. You have stifled the people and their will. Why do you think this civilization is faltering so badly? God granted us a free will. Here, you are trying to take it away."

"But what if they are unworthy?" Another council member asks.

"They are to be held to the same standards as any Gregorian. Do not stop someone just because they are not Gregorian. And, for God's sake, let the people live!" The Prince's eyes clear to show his crystal blue eyes again.

"And what if they will not conform?" A council member asks.

"You already have immigration laws that are well enforced but you have not allowed these legal immigrants to become Gregorians. I will remind you that my own ancestor was the first High Priestess to the Holy Temple before the Anarchy Wars. She was not Gregorian."

"You are right my grandson." The Gregorian Larch stands. "The changes were made after the Anarchy Wars when the church had to take over the Gregorian government in order to prevent a total collapse of our civilization. It may be about time for some of these laws and regulations to be rescinded."

"When? You need help now and this is the only way you will get it." Prince Marckolius forcefully states.

"I will start right now. Both Viktorlo and Brianto, come forward to me."

Both release the guards and walk forward, placing their hands in the hands of the Gregorian Larch.

"You both have passed all of the tests in both knowledge and skill. Doing so shows us all that God has led you to us to become more than what you are. I bless your hands so you may depart God's blessings upon all." He places his hands on their foreheads. "I bless your minds so you may continue to be guided by God." He places his hands on their chests and then their lips. "You are now Brothers in the Church. State your designation."

"Warrior Priests!" both exclaim.

"So be it, you are both now Brother Viktorlo and Brother Brianto. Both are now Warrior Priests and have all of the rights and privileges due your levels. Go in peace and serve God."

Both bow slightly and then back away to stand behind Prince Marckolius.

"We accept your request for us to take care of the situation. We will have this resolved within the next week. I do hope that this Council will reach out and work with our allies to develop an alternate fuel source for the long-term advancement of all. I will remind you that this is only a stopgap measure. My uncle will interfere again in the future." Marckolius bows slightly to his grandfather.

"Grandson, please be careful. Remember, God is watching."

"This Council would be wise to remember the same. Until the next time grandfather," Prince Marckolius bows to his Grandfather before turning and entering the elevator with Viktorlo and Brianto. The elevator doors close.

Chapter 5

The mission

PRINCE MARCKOLIUS, VIKTORLO, AND BRIANTO settle into a very large lavishly furnished cabin. Pastries, bottles of wine, and large plates of fruit are set up in a buffet style spread. The vibrant oranges, yellows, reds, and assorted florescent colors of the fruit catch their eyes. The smell of citric and sugar fills the entire cabin.

"You booked us a private yacht?" Viktorlo barely gets the question out as he bites into a bright orange apple looking fruit.

"It's part of our birthday celebration."

"Where are the women?" Brianto jokes as he eats a purple jelly filled pastry.

"Funny! It's not that type of celebration."

Viktorlo bumps Brianto over, "Why? Didn't we get permission to do whatever we want?"

"Only as part of the mission," Prince Marckolius seriously answers as he locks the cabin door. "Just eat and drink up."

After a while, all three collapse onto the extremely large bed. All three nap for a while before waking up.

Once all three are fully awake Prince Marckolius pulls a glistening silver ball from a small pack. He pulls out a small tripod and sets the ball on the tripod in the middle of the room. He presses the top. A female voice echoes throughout the room, "Scanning . . ." Brianto and Viktorlo remain on the bed as red and green lights flicker throughout. "All surveillance devices deactivated, sealing the room." After a short pause the female voice proclaims, "The room is sealed."

"Good," Prince Marckolius pulls out a thick silver plate. He places it on the top of the silver ball. The plate automatically balances itself. "We are now ready to start the briefing."

"Need movie refreshments." Brianto jokes.

Both Brianto and Viktorlo grab an open bottle and sit back down on the bed.

"Yes, well let's begin." Prince Marckolius taps the plate and a 3D image of a hairy man beast projects above. "This is Osserate. He is the current head of the Syndicate. He is sometimes referred to as Lord Osserate and General Osserate. He was once a General in the Intican Alliance. That light green stone around his neck is a Demon Stone. It allows him to take on the characteristics and abilities of the demon encased in the stone."

"Very nice, I'm glad I'm not the one fighting him," Viktorlo snickers.

Two more images appear in place of the image of Osserate. "These two are his right and left hand thugs. They are the first to die," both Brianto and Viktorlo chuckle. "They never leave Osserate's side. There are plenty more Intican there, most were brought in by Osserate as they retired or left the Intican Alliance. They are seasoned fighters."

"Is there a plan to kill them off?" Viktorlo asks. "Strategically speaking, we really need a plan to kill those things off."

"I was going to leave that up to you to figure out. Remember as you so plainly stated, you're not the one fighting Osserate." The image projection changes to that of a beautiful glistening woman with long darkish red hair and a light round face. Both Brianto and Viktorlo whistle at the image. "Yeah, yeah, control yourselves. This is Anna. She is second in charge of the Syndicate."

"She is not a normal looking vampire," comments Brianto.

"Nope, she was originally a Eugenitor."

"How?" Viktorlo asks with great surprise. "Eugenitors are immune to the blood disease."

"I have no idea and no one else seems to know either so we are moving on." The 3D image changes to two vampire women. The Prince points to right one with long blond hair and soft facial features, "This is Telibina." He points at the one on the left with short dark hair and dark tan skin, "This is Darling. They are Anna's assistants. Anna rarely goes anywhere without them."

Brianto finishes the bottle he is drinking out of, "Now that's an interesting picture."

"I am still concerned about the situation with the Intican there?" Viktorlo takes big gulps from the bottle in his hand.

"As I said you need to work out a plan to take care of it. Mind you, vampires hate the Intican. That hatred goes back thousands of years, back to when the Intican were werewolves. The vampires should help fight against them. Just remember though, that none of the vampires can be within six meters of you two and still fight. You will need to coordinate the taking down of the other Intican with Telibina and Darling."

"Do they go splat like most of the other races?" Viktorlo finishes his bottle.

"Sorry, no. You should remember from that ice ball we were on many years ago. You are going to have to take their heads off to make sure they stay dead. Intican do heal quickly so the sooner you can decapitate them the better." The image changes to a plump older man with a short white beard. "This is Ambassador Jonathan. If you both remember, my father believes he has been cheating our family out of contract payments and dues using a nefarious set of accounting gimmicks and contract stipulations. We pull his financials and pass codes to his accounts to conduct a full investigation. He has amassed a fortune that rivals some of the lower families. The Ambassador is listed as having a biodroid traveling companion."

"I hate biodroids!" Viktorlo gets up and start looking for another bottle.

"Biodroids are illegal but the authorities have likely been paid off for the waiver he has for it. When we get close to him we can hopefully scan him and find out the truth to a lot of questions."

"Is this briefing done? I'm out of drink." Brianto gets off the bed and starts searching for another bottle too.

"Hold on," Viktorlo looks hard at the label on the bottle he is holding. "I'm not drunk or anything. There's no buzz."

"Hey, neither am I."

Prince Marckolius lightly chuckles while he takes the silver plate off the silver ball. The 3D image disappears.

"You didn't think I ordered real alcohol, did you?" The Prince looks at their scowling faces. "I guess you did. Just remember, we are on a mission. We do not want to ingest anything that could impair our faculties."

A gurgling sound comes from Viktorlo. "Oh no, we've been drinking high protein drinks." He barely finishes as he goes running to the oversized bathroom.

"But I thought protein drinks taste like gruel?"

"No, they just make it taste like that during the training. It can be made to taste like whatever we want. In this case I ordered it to taste like Con Se Migliori Wine. It did taste good, right?"

"I couldn't tell the difference till now. Wait until I'm done in here. I am going to kick your ass!" Viktorlo shouts from inside the bathroom.

"I wanted to mention that we need to covertly get the Ambassador's financials without him knowing. Once we are on Desespero whatever happens to him happens."

Prince Marckolius taps the silver ball. A small beep and "The room is now insecure," echo throughout the room. He picks up the ball and tripod and places them back in the pack.

"We should be dropping out of Interdimensional Space soon."

Brianto starts banging on the wall to the bathroom. "Aren't you done yet?"

"You both know that stuff goes right through me."

Prince Marckolius hits the unlock button on the control panel next to the door. The light changes from red to green. He hits the open button but nothing happens. He hits it several more times with nothing happening.

"Ummmmm, you think something is up again?" Brianto plops down on the bed almost exasperated. "I am really getting sick of idiots trying shit with us."

Viktorlo walks out of the bathroom and pushes Prince Marckolius. "You know that stuff goes right through me. You could have given me a warning!"

"I slipped you the pill for it early on; otherwise, it would have kicked in long ago," the Prince chuckles.

"Anyways Viktorlo, we are locked in." Brianto sings.

"Oh come on!" Viktorlo shakes his head.

Prince Marckolius rolls his eyes and shakes his head. "Let me try the steward and bridge before we jump to conclusions." He hits the intercom button on the panel, "Hello, anyone there?" There is no response. He presses down on the emergency button, no response again.

"Now may we jump to our conclusions?" Viktorlo rhetorically voices.

"You know," Brianto begins, "one would think that given the number of idiots and morons we have dispatched the next batch would think twice about trying to kill us or kidnap us."

"Yeah, I know!"

"Okay, take out your magic blue crystal and open the fracken' door." Viktorlo angrily points at the door controls.

"No, no, I got this." Brianto hops off the bed and walks over to the wall next to the door. "These older yachts have a closed circuit for their emergency escape system. If the power goes out the door would automatically open. The conduit runs along the floor." In one smooth motion, Brianto pulls out his battle-ax slicing into the lower panel of the wall. He pulls it away with the panel wedged onto the blade. The panel drops to the floor with a muffled clank. "Now all I have to do is slice the orange conduit in half to break the circuit to open the door." The battle-ax swishes through the air cutting the conduit and the cabling in half. With an even louder clank and rattle the door unlocks and slides partially open, "Tada!"

"He actually did it." An astonished Viktorlo walks up to the door to pier out into the hallway. "No one is out there at all."

"Well, what do you want to do?" Brianto pushes the door the rest of the way.

"Let's make our way up to the bridge." Prince Marckolius suggests.

As all three make their way up to the bridge of the yacht, they pass several smaller open compartments. They stop and look in each one to find no one. They stop at the final open door before the closed doors of the bridge to find several bodies.

"I think this was the captain." Viktorlo says kneeling down.

Brianto checks out the other bodies. "Here is the steward, cook, and cleaning person."

"We need to say a few words so please bow your heads." All three bow, "May their souls, through the mercy of God, rest in peace."

"Amen."

"Amen."

They silently close the door and stare at the double doors leading to the bridge, their eyes glowing bright red.

"Reach in there with your minds." Prince Marckolius instructs. "How many do you see?"

"I see three men."

"I see them." Viktorlo places his hands on the doors. "They are dark. There is one on each side of the door"

"Very good, I will take the first officer."

Prince Marckolius pulls the control panel off the wall. He reaches into the wall with his blue crystal. They hear the click of the door lock releasing. The doors slide open to show the first officer popping up from the captain's chair.

Prince Marckolius enters first with Brianto and Viktorlo following close behind.

"Order your friends to put down their weapons, my Prince." The first officer pulls a large handgun from his holster and points it at the Prince. "My orders are to simply stop you from meeting up with the Ambassador and arriving at Desespero. None of you three need be hurt. You are quite safe my Prince."

"I can see that by the bodies in the other room." Prince Marckolius retorts.

"Tell your friends to lay down their weapons. The contract only covers you, not them. If you don't want them harmed then tell them to lay down their weapons." Anxiety creeps into the first officer's voice as his eyes lock on the red pulsing hue of the Prince's eyes. "Please my Prince . . ."

"Brianto, Viktorlo, your weapons, please embed them in the men."

"No, hand them to the . . ."

Before the first officer could finish, both his men explode as the blades of the weapons hit bone. Blood drips from the ceiling and runs down the back wall of the bridge. A puddle of blood forms at Viktorlo's and Brianto's feet with a strong smell of iron permeating the air. Prince Marckolius walks forward and takes the handgun from the first officer's clammy wet hands. The Prince looks him square in the eyes. Fear is all the first officer feels.

"Who is the contract with?" The Prince asks in a whisper.

"Yoooooouuuur uuuuunnnnnkkle!"

"I see. What is the code to unlock the controls?"

"None," the first officer tries to fight the words coming from his mouth. "Only a key is required."

"Please hand me the key," the Prince continues in a whispery tone.

The first officer reaches into his pocket and pulls out a small brown crystal on a neck chain. The Prince takes it from him and hands it to Viktorlo. Both Brianto and Viktorlo sit in the driver's chairs. Viktorlo inserts the key. The controls immediately light up and release the drive wheels.

"Where do we want to go?" Viktorlo asks.

"Set the course for Desespero. Now my new friend, you have committed treason under the law. As the Crown Prince, I have the authority to decide your fate. What would be a suitable fate for you?"

Brianto pipes up, "Death is the only sentence I have ever heard be given out for treason."

"Mmmmmmmm, good point Brianto, I don't normally follow tradition, but, in this case, I think I will."

"No, please my Prince. I know I can provide more information." Fear drips from every word.

"You have nothing!"

"Please have mercy on me."

The Prince slaps the first officer. He flies across the small bridge landing in the corner between the navigator's chair and the metal wall.

"You dare!" The Prince begins in a loud angry voice. "You dare ask for mercy? What about the dead in the other room? Were they granted mercy?"

"They wouldn't cooperate and I had a contract I had to fulfill." The first officer blurts out as he wipes blood from his mouth.

"There will be no mercy granted here this day for such mercy can only come from God after you meet Him. You will be punished by the most ardent means I know of, the exact opposite of mercy!"

The Prince walks over and grabs the first officer by his neck. He wrenches him upward holding him in the air without choking him.

"Your sentence for treason is death! Brianto, please make sure the dead bodies have nothing on them that he can use to injure himself."

Brianto gets up and leaves the bridge. The first officer remains dangling from Prince Marckolius' left hand.

Brianto returns after a few minutes, "I have removed all of the belts and anything sharp and pointy from the room."

"Would you please strip our friend here?"

"You're serious? Viktorlo, are you just going to sit there?" Brianto asks in disbelief.

"I'm flying the ship. The Prince's punishment is actually rather amusing."

Brianto shakes his head as he walks over to the Prince and the dangling first officer. He proceeds to rip off the officer's clothes and boots leaving him with only his underwear on. "You don't want me to remove those too, do you?"

"No. Thank you my friend. If you will excuse us," Prince Marckolius leaves the bridge still holding the man. He hits the open button on the door to the room with the dead bodies, and tosses the officer into the room. "You get to stay here with the bodies of your victims until we land."

The door to the room shuts and locks. The Prince rips the controls off the wall, leaving the panel hanging by a partial cable. The corridors echo with the sound of the first officer banging on the door and crying out. The Prince turns and walks into the bridge, hitting the close button as he passes. The doors muffle the sounds coming from the first officer.

Both Brianto and Viktorlo look up at the Prince from the drivers' chairs. The Prince sits down in the captain's chair, letting out a loud sigh. His eyes clear to show pure crystal blue.

"What are you going to do with him once we are on Desespero?" Brianto asks.

"The simple answer is vampires." Viktorlo answers.

"Vampires?"

"Vampires," Viktorlo chuckles.

"I don't get it, vampires?"

"You'll see when we get there. There's nothing like death by vampire." Viktorlo continues chuckling.

"Oh," Brianto looks blankly at Viktorlo until, "OH! You mean the slow pain of death as every drop of blood is vacuumed out of the body while the heart beats harder and harder to keep the person alive, both mentally and physically painful."

"All right, when will we be arriving at Desespero?" Asks the Prince.

"Lucky for us he was only flying this yacht at quarter speed. We will be there in a few hours, actually beating the Ambassador." Viktorlo explains.

"Good. Brianto please put some music on or something to drown out that idiot's noise making."

Brianto finds some classical music in the system. As the music plays through the bridge speakers Brianto turns and asks, "Do vampires have fleas?"

Both the Prince and Viktorlo look at each other before busting out laughing.

"No, I mean it. Do vampires have fleas?"

"After everything we just went through and you ask a silly question like that? Think about the question," Prince Marckolius begins. "Anything that bites a vampire, including bugs, dies in seconds if not milliseconds."

"I'm almost afraid to ask why you are asking that question." Viktorlo briefly stops laughing.

"Well, just in case . . . You know."

"You pervert!" The Prince busts out laughing even harder. "You mean to . . ."

"Like you two never thought about it? Telibina is one cute vampire."

Viktorlo barely gets the words out, "He's got the 'hots' for a vampire."

The Prince stops laughing, "You're serious. Unless you are going to ask one of them, I believe you are just going to have to take my word for it or find out for yourself."

"Fine, I will do just that."

"Pervert!" Viktorlo turns back to the controls.

"You know what, this trip just got better." Brianto turns back with a smile.

"Can we put this silliness aside and focus on the mission?" The Prince sits back in the captain's chair. "What am I ever going to do with you two?"

CHAPTER 6

YOU HAVE A FUNNY WAY OF NEGOTIATING CONTRACTS

THE YACHT TOUCHES DOWN LETTING off steam vapors as the hull cools. It is a typical gloomy day on Desespero. The wind blows across the landing pad taking away the vapors from the hull. Three vampires in dark green jumpsuits run up to the ship and stand at attention waiting for the occupants to depart.

The side doors open, stairs slide down to the landing pad from underneath, the Prince and his friends disembark. As they walk onto the concrete of the landing pad, the vampire's images change with their previous image blowing away like sand in the wind.

"I take you are the cleaning crew?" The Prince politely asks.

"Yes Sir," all three bow slightly as they answer in unison.

"The room just outside of the bridge has several dead bodies, prepare them to be returned to their families. The bridge needs a special cleaning. As a bonus to you three, there is a freshy in the room with the dead bodies. Do as you want with the freshy."

"Thank you my Prince." All three say as they rush up into yacht.

"Now that's enthusiasm!" Viktorlo points out.

They walk towards the large stone castle. The castle walls are several stories high with parapets and towers that protrude up many stories higher. High power weapons are visible in the towers and along the walls of the castle.

"They do know we are coming, right?" Brianto's concern echoes on Viktorlo's face.

"We sent them the message. The cleaning crew knew we were coming. Look, here they come." The Prince points to the large entrance to the castle from the landing pad.

The Prince and his friends see a small group approaching them. They meet Anna and her two assistants' midway. Their images blow away from them as they come closer.

"My Prince," Anna bows, "I am Anna and this is Telibina and Darling." Anna hugs the Prince. "It has been about eight years?"

"Yes it has. This is Viktorlo and Brianto." Prince Marckolius gestures to them.

"Osserate is still away and will not be here till morning. The Ambassador should be arriving in several hours or so." Anna explains. "I thought you were meeting the Ambassador?"

"Our travel plans changed."

"I see. Our cleaning crew's orders were quite telling. We should get you settled." Anna gestures toward the castle. "We will have dinner ready in about an hour. Our kitchen has plenty of food and wine since we have Intican here." She finishes with disdain.

As they walk to the castle, Anna wraps her right arm around the Prince's left arm. She leans in to him, "I've been following your exploits over these last many years. You've developed somewhat of a reputation."

"Reputation?" The Prince thinks to himself, *'She really smells good!'*

'She's a vampire. Focus . . .' The Prince hears in his mind.

"Ever since you killed that Intican on that ice ball I have been counting down when you would be coming here. You are going to kill Osserate, right?"

"That is the plan. But we should talk about this in private with the others present."

"Are you always hot to the touch? I mean you seem to be running a high fever. You poor dear, we are going to have to do something about that."

Once inside the castle the group enters a secluded dining room where they eat and discuss their plan.

"You three need to rest before the Ambassador arrives. The Prince and I need to discuss a few other contract details. If you will excuse us," Anna stands up to go.

"The contract she is talking about is the contract for the capturing of two of the Duad Bantam so we can practice on the real thing," the Prince explains.

"But your aunt isn't going to like it." Viktorlo pipes up.

"Never mind that, what she doesn't know won't hurt any of us." Brianto jokes.

"She will eventually and when she does you will have to explain. However, until then, practice, practice, practice! With what you three have been through I am sure she will forgive but never forget." Anna pulls on Marckolius' arm to leave the room, almost dragging him.

They arrive at Anna's room, "Come on in. I just need to get your account information for the contract deposit."

The suite is very luxurious with bright red and purple bedding on the king size bed. The Prince sits in one of the red and purple oversized chairs to relax while Anna disappears into a side room. She comes back out with papers and wearing a velvet red robe matching her long red hair.

"These are the papers for the contract deposit. Standard stuff . . ."

The Prince takes the papers. While looking at them Anna places her hand on his forehead.

"You poor dear, you are really hot. Your blood must be boiling."

"I have always been hotter than everyone else. It's been attributed to my high metabolism."

She places her hands on his cheeks, "Your blood is so hot. You are going to burn up if you don't cool down. Here, let me help you." Anna pulls the Prince from the chair. The slight height difference allows her to look down at him. Her glistening skin reflects the lighting of the room. "What you need is a soothing bath to cool you down."

"Bath?"

"You have heard of a bath before, right?"

"Well, sort of."

"You have been so sheltered." Anna looks exasperated at the Prince. "Come on. This will relax and cool you."

Anna grabs his right hand and leads him to a marble tiled room with a pool. Soap bubbles with a scent of lavender float upward.

"Strip down and get in."

'You aren't thinking of doing this?' Echoes in his mind as the Prince sees Anna taking off her robe and clothes.

'I think I will.'

Several hours pass before the Ambassador arrives with his servant. The Prince, Viktorlo, and Brianto receive the notification and assemble quickly in the hall near the Ambassador's quarters.

"Rested?" Viktorlo asks.

"That was most interesting and fun," Brianto chuckles.

"If you two are wondering, I have gained Anna's trust. She really trusts Telibina and Darling."

"Darling is a fantastic, but she's just not my type. I'd like something more exotic."

Brianto and Prince Marckolius both stop, turn, and look at Viktorlo. Their disbelieving look of surprise is very visible.

"What is more exotic than a vampire anyways?" Brianto blurts out.

"I don't know. I'm just not attracted to vampires."

"Maybe you would prefer an Intican or a Felini?"

"Shhhh, both of you, pay attention, we are almost there," The Prince motions putting his right index finger over his mouth.

"Oh yeah, I have an answer to our question," Brianto continues, "Vampires do not have fleas."

"You are still stuck on that? And that was your question, not ours." Viktorlo corrects.

"I said SHHHHHHHHHHHHHHHHH!"

Upon approach the images of the two vampires standing guard fall away to show their natural race.

"Both of you, stay out here to prevent anyone from interfering," The Prince orders.

Both nod as they back away from the three of them.

"I can't open this door. The stone work is far too thick." Brianto jokes.

The Prince places his hand on the door control sensor. The sensor emits a green pulse of light.

"Open." The door opens for the Prince upon command. "All of my family's castles and compounds have these programmed sensors installed. Since I am registered as the Crown Prince, I can open any door in this castle. After all, the Syndicate leases the castle from us so I am technically the landlord."

"That's funny your father is the landlord. That makes you just the representative or something like that," Brianto points out.

"The Ambassador should be asleep," the Prince leads them into the room. The room layout is simple with a secluded bedroom off the living room.

"I've seen better décor in a hotel room," Comments Viktorlo.

"Shhhhh!" Prince Marckolius waves at Brianto and Viktorlo to be quiet. "Just find his storage crystal so we can get out of here before his biodroid wakes up." He whispers.

"Ambassador, we have visitors!" A male voice pieces the darkness of the room.

The Prince looks in the direction of the voice and sees two whitish glowing eyes looking out from the dark bedroom. "Fracken' biodroid!"

The lights come on throughout the room. The Ambassador pushes the biodroid aside and enters wearing an oversized dark blue robe and slippers.

"Get out! It's late and I'm tired," barks the Ambassador.

Prince Marckolius steps forward toward the Ambassador with his hands folded in front of him, "I needed to speak with you about the contract negotiations later today. Since we . . . ."

"I don't know who you think you are but I will make sure you are forcibly removed if need be! Now get out!"

"He doesn't recognize him." Viktorlo whispers to Brianto.

"This should be good!" Brianto responds.

"Since we did not rendezvous as scheduled yesterday I thought we could catch up now."

The Ambassador stops moving and talking, he only looks at the Prince with his very dark brown eyes wide open.

"Yes, that is right Ambassador, I am Prince Marckolius." The Prince turns slightly and gestures to Brianto and Viktorlo, "They accompany me on my travels and missions."

Brianto leans into the Prince, "Maybe you should release him?"

"I'm not doing anything. I think he's scared to the point he can't talk or move."

"I'm not either," pipes up Viktorlo. "I think he's got issues."

The Prince wakes up the Ambassador, "Are you alright?"

The Ambassador backs away to the cold stone wall, "You aren't supposed to be here."

"Yes, well here we are. Anyways, how would you know if we were or weren't supposed be here?" After a short pause, "You are going to answer the question."

"Get out or you will be very sorry!" The Ambassador threatens.

The Prince's eyes develop a red hue as he walks up to the Ambassador, stopping mere centimeters from their noses touching. "You dare threaten your Prince? I take great exception to such actions."

"Wow, he seems much calmer than usual," Brianto comments.

"I agree he does seem much calmer. Normally he would have already frozen him or something worse," Viktorlo walks forward a few steps.

"Andro!" The Ambassador yells out. The biodroid walks out of the bedroom holding two swords. "Kill . . ." The Ambassador gurgles.

The biodroid leaps at the Prince. Both Viktorlo and Brianto block it, throwing it back into the bedroom. Viktorlo pulls out both of his swords and thrusts them into the upper torso of the biodroid. Brianto plants his battle-ax into the biodroid's head. Viktorlo continues cutting up the biodroid until it stops thrashing about on the floor. The florescent fluid used as blood splashes throughout the bedroom.

The Prince looks at the Ambassador's face to see a look of shock. "You didn't even see Viktorlo and Brianto move did you?"

"No." The Ambassador hangs his head.

"You see the cameras in the corners of the room? They are recording everything. They have recorded you committing treason. Now then, let's discuss the location of your storage crystal."

The Prince stares into the Ambassador's eyes, "You will tell me everything, including the location of your vaults and associated combinations. How about including my uncle's secret vault locations as well? I do hope you choose to cooperate with our investigation. If you choose not to then I will have to render punishment."

"You're just as demented and evil as your uncle. I will tell you nothing." The Prince grabs the Ambassador's hand and thrusts it in front of his face just as the Ambassador attempts to spit at him.

"Your every thought and movement is telegraphed before you do it. I guess this is going to be quite painful for you." The Prince turns to Brianto, "Have one of the guards get me an airtight box about the size of the Ambassador's head." The Prince turns back to the Ambassador, "Shall we begin?"

A couple hours later, the Prince and his two friends leave the room. The Prince is carrying a large blackish box with a silver bow on top.

The Prince turns to the two guards, "Be sure to clean up the mess in there. Incinerate what's left of the biodroid and the Ambassador."

The two guards bow slightly as the Prince and his friends walk down the dimly lit hallway.

"Viktorlo, are you alright?" Prince Marckolius calmly asks.

"I will be fine. I really hate biodroids. They give me the creeps."

Brianto silently pats Viktorlo on his back.

"Let's get going. Osserate should be in the cantina by now eating breakfast."

"We'll meet up with Telibina and Darling to do our part." Brianto grabs Viktorlo.

They separate, allowing the Prince to enter the main hall of the castle alone. He continues to walk through the great hall and into the cantina, passing very few vampires along the way. Upon entering the cantina, the Prince sees Osserate sitting in a far secluded corner with his two bodyguards at a round table.

The Prince takes a deep breath before walking over to the bar area. The vampire behind the bar keeps his distance as he slides an orange breakfast drink down to him. The Prince grabs the drink with his free hand. He turns and walks over to the table where Osserate is sitting at. He pulls the empty chair out with his foot while placing the box and his drink down on the table.

"You don't mind if I join you, do you?" The Prince stares at Osserate before sitting down.

"Sure, why not. You have some type of gumption." Osserate responds. "Our meeting isn't supposed to take place for another hour or so."

"I was thirsty. Seeing you sitting here I thought I would come over and introduce myself." The Prince stares at the dark green stone around Osserate's neck.

"I know who you are, no need for introductions." Osserate finishes his drink. "Hmmm, I wonder what you have been up to since arriving here."

"What does it matter to you?"

Osserate sniffs the air, "I smell the stench of Anna all over you."

The Prince finishes his drink. "I brought you a gift. I was taught that it was customary to exchange gifts at the beginning of contract negotiations."

"And here I have nothing to give in exchange."

The Prince pushes the box to the center of the table. "I don't mind. The idea is to create good will and trust."

"Ahhh, my Prince, you give and give without expecting anything but good will? I find that very hard to believe."

"I expect you to accept the gift in the spirit it is given." The Prince smiles broadly. "Go ahead, take the box and open it."

"Maybe I should wait for the Ambassador to join us."

"I'm afraid the Ambassador won't be joining us. He has fallen very ill."

"Oh my, then maybe we should post pone our meeting?"

"No need, my father has given me the authority to negotiate for the Proprietorship."

"Well then," Osserate laughs, "you will be schooled by the best. Let's open that gift." Osserate shakes the box "Sounds squishy." He pulls the ribbon off the box as he looks at the smiling Prince. Osserate pops open the top. His associates gasp. He looks down into the box to see the head of the Ambassador. "I see you have a sense of humor."

"Humor has nothing to do with it" The Prince notices Osserate's two associates squirming a little. "I know you like these types of gifts."

The Prince unclips his sword from his belt. Osserate continues to stare at the Prince with his yellowish eyes. His hair stands on end. In the blink of an eye, the Prince flips the table on end toward Osserate with his left hand as he stands. The sword in his right hand swings to the right cutting off the head of the Intican. The Prince continues the spin with a swirling grace, cutting off the head of the second Intican. Both of Osserate's associates are dead.

Osserate rises, sliding straight back to the stone wall. Everyone clears out of the cantina in record speed. The Prince points his sword at Osserate, the red hue of his eyes pulsing with every heartbeat.

"You, my friend, are going to die for this." Snarls Osserate.

Osserate grabs the stone with both hands. His yellow eyes turn green. The beast's hair thickens and the nose lengthens to that of an animal. The Prince stands back and stares, waiting for the transformation to complete.

'Revenge is the prevue of God,' echoes through the Prince's head.

The Prince smiles, *'God has given me a great gift. Who am I to refuse it?'*

Osserate kicks the table at the Prince. The Prince ducks out of the way. He looks up to see Osserate bearing down on him, teeth and claws at the ready. The Prince swings his sword nicking Osserate's leg. Osserate howls openly as the wound and hair on his leg burns with fire.

"Using the demon stone opens you up to someone like me who uses a sacramental as a sword." Prince Marckolius taunts. "You might be as fast as me but you are far clumsier." The Prince ducks repeatedly, avoiding Osserate's claws.

"You foolish boy," Osserate yells as he charges, "I will not stop until you are dead!"

The Prince slips on some spilled drinks. Osserate reaches to grab the Prince but the Prince's sword severs Osserate's outstretched arm. Osserate howls in pain, stumbling backwards and crushing the empty tables and chairs. He throws the wooden pieces at the Prince as the stump smolders. The Prince ducks behind the bar, dodging each piece. Osserate's severed arm catches fire on the ground. The Prince runs out from behind the bar grabbing the flaming arm. He throws it at Osserate, catching his attention. The Prince's sword slices through the air cutting off the dark green stone necklace from around Osserate's neck. The Prince jumps over Osserate destroying the stone with his sword.

The Prince stands back to watch as Osserate thrashes about while transforming back into a normal Intican. The green eyes turn back to yellow. The animal face and nose are once again more of a human hair covered face. The claws and teeth retract. All the while Osserate howls in pain. A green mist flows from his mouth and nostrils dissipating above him. Blood pours from his wounds.

"If I gave you enough time you might heal. So you understand why I can't let you."

"Please, I can tell you things. I have information you will want." Osserate pleads.

The Prince brushes off the last of the splinters of wood thrown at him. "What can you tell me that I don't already know?"

"I can help prove your uncle was behind the death contract on your mother."

"I already know that."

"But I can give you a copy of the contract. Please spare me and I will give you everything. Even the secret vault belonging to your uncle in the deep dungeon is yours."

"Thank you Osserate but that isn't going to change anything. Your time as head of the Syndicate is over." Prince Marckolius swings his sword cleanly cutting off Osserate's head.

The Prince takes another deep breath, letting out a great sigh. He grabs the head as he walks out of the cantina. Brianto meets him in the great hall and hands him a long pike. Corpses of both vampires and beheaded Intican lay about. The Prince walks out into the courtyard leaving a trail of blood from Osserate's severed head. Viktorlo joins Brianto at the courtyard entrance. They stand there watching the Prince place the pike in the center of the courtyard. He forces Osserate's head onto the pike.

Anna joins Prince Marckolius. She places her hand on his back, "You have a funny way of negotiating contracts." She chuckles. "I like it!"

"It's still not over. My uncle is still out there. His power and fortune will now diminish. We will empty every vault the Ambassador and my uncle are tied to. I don't know why they have been stock piling all that money and gold but I am going to find out."

"But for now, you need to clean up and rest. We will pamper your friends beyond their dreams. You three are heroes to the others. You have rid us of the Intican and their influences. You will always be thought of as our friend and ally." Anna turns the Prince away from the head on the pike. "Come, it's time you rested."

CHAPTER 7

A SET OF TRASH HEAPS

MONTHS PASS BEFORE THE PRINCE and his friends arrive back on Propri traveling aboard a royal cruiser. Men unload crate after crate after crate from the cargo holds of the ship. The Prince and his friends stand by watching ever so closely. The private landing pad next to the Palace allows them to unload the ship in private.

Once the cruiser is unloaded, they accompany the cargo down to the massive vaults under the Palace. The King and his guards stand by the entrance. Prince Marckolius meets his father and bows slightly to him.

"Morning father," They hug, "You are looking well."

The King pats his son on the back, "You pulled off a lot while you were gone. And you have been gone a very long time."

"We needed to settle the situation governing the Syndicate and other financials from the removing of Ambassador Jonathan and Osserate." Prince Marckolius explains. "We managed to retrieve most, if not all, of the embezzled funds and contract kickbacks from our Ambassador."

Crates continuously stream pass the King and Prince. The King puts out his hand and the crates stop.

"Open it." The King commands.

"The crates are magnetically sealed with bio locks." The Prince walks up and places his thumb on the locking plate.

The top pops up. The guards immediately grab each corner and lift the top away from the King and Prince. Both look in to see bars of pure gold.

"Feel free to have any of the crates opened father. Each crate is full of gold, jewels, and other precious metals. We even found secret accounts worth billions of credits. The Ambassador was colluding with Osserate to defraud and embezzle from all of the families of the Proprietorship, not just ours."

"How many crates did you bring?" The King's eyes are wide with astonishment.

"Twenty-three crates after we took our customary recovery fee."

"What about Osserate's accounts?" A wide smile spreads across the King's face.

"The money was embezzled from the Syndicate. That amount was inconsequential to what was embezzled from the Proprietorship." The Prince points to the guards, "Reseal the crate and move on. Let's get these crates into vaults."

"Come, you can leave your friends to oversee this. We have much to discuss."

They enter a plush elevator. Once the guards enter, the elevator ascends. The King gives the Prince another hug.

"You have done far better than I had hoped. It's my thought a grand ball should be thrown in your honor."

"It wasn't just me father, Viktorlo and Brianto helped immensely. I already gave them a cut." The King looks at him with a blank stare. "The cut came from the recovery fee, not out of the overall total amount recovered."

"You paid them from your own pocket?"

The Prince grabs his father's hand, with a flash the King and Prince stand in an empty elevator.

"We now have some privacy." The Prince starts, "One of the guards seems to be listening far too intensely."

The King shows some disorientation, "Where are we?"

"No need to fret father, we are in a kind of in between place, mentally connected so we can have a quick private conversation. Didn't mother ever do this with you?"

"Yes but that was her and it has been a very long time."

"Well, she used to share stories with me all the time this way. Teachings and mental training easy and quick because what happens here may seem like minutes while in reality it may only be seconds.

Our minds can process information far faster than the input and output of our bodies."

"I know the premise behind it. Now then, what exactly went on while you were off for three months?"

"We were collecting the accounts and contents of the vaults the Ambassador had setup in some very interesting and not so nice places. Some of those places do not exist anymore. We cleared out six vaults and four secret bank accounts. Viktorlo really has a knack for gathering intelligence and deciphering codes."

"Did the Ambassador share any of these vaults with anyone?"

"Osserate on a couple of them and an unnamed person on others, the sharing was more of a joint or partnership type with aliases and front companies. What took so long was following up on two other vaults he seemed to have moved the contents of a while back. One issue though, we believe my uncle has something to do with several of the front companies."

"Never mind your uncle, what about the contracts you negotiated? You handled the contracts for both the Proprietorship and Gregoria with the Syndicate."

"What do you mean, never mind my uncle?" The Prince looks surprised.

"I will handle looking into your uncle. What about replacing Osserate with Anna?"

"I trust Anna. She will be a great partner. The contracts are simple. The Syndicate will pick up the processed fuel waste from the entire Proprietorship, which is quite a lot. They then ship the waste to Gregoria who reprocesses it into the fuel they use. It's a win-win contract. We get our percentage of the contract in taxes and fees and the Syndicate makes even more money by selling the waste, which means we get even more in taxes and fees coming into the treasury." The Prince sounds jubilant.

"Since you negotiated both contracts, don't you get a percentage?"

"I get one solitary percent of the contract between the Proprietorship and the Syndicate. I do get about ten percent of the contract between the Syndicate and Gregoria."

"I see, but there were no reports of any other large deposits into our treasury account. You don't have any secret accounts, do you?"

"I thought having secret accounts and slush funds were a hereditary trait. A family tradition I am happy to carry to on."

The King hugs the Prince, "I am so proud of you! You have learned everything I have been trying to teach you over these many years."

"Yes father, I have learned that pure Capitalism requires creative contract negotiating."

"Your progression is astonishing. Unfortunately, once we reach the war room your uncle will be there. He is still quite upset about you commandeering the royal cruiser that was supposed to pick him up. On top of that, he continuously tried to piece together where you were going without much success. Some of the places caused him concern but I was thinking the concern was for your safety and nothing more."

"The only safety he cares about is his own. Like I said before, we believed that . . ."

"Now, now Marckolius," The Kings pats him on the back. "You should know that he was very concerned about your wellbeing. I don't think I have ever seen him quite like that before."

"You must be joking! He's been behind most of the kidnappings and other attempts on my life."

The King looks angrily at the Prince, "You listen to me, he has your best interests at heart. If I thought for one moment he was behind any of it, do you think I wouldn't take action?"

"I guess." The Prince pauses for a moment, "We are almost there."

The Prince lets go of his father's hand and steadies him. The elevator stops to open in a large round multi-step room. In the center is a large round table with holographic projections of planets and ships. Standing off to side is Duke Yoritus with several uniformed officers. All exit the elevator. The guards take up position around the top step of the room. The King and Prince walk to the center. The Prince stands across from his scowling uncle.

"I have a few choice words for you boy!" Duke Yoritus starts, "Gallivanting all over two galaxies with your friends on some type of joy ride with the royal cruiser that was supposed to pick me up from a very important mission."

"My dearest uncle, did you not know that we were recovering the embezzled funds that once belonged to Ambassador Jonathan?" The Prince asks.

The Duke slams his fist down on the holographic table. "You had no right to put yourself into danger like that."

"Stop the arguing now!" The King yells.

"You are acting as if we took something that belonged to you. What we did was confiscate and recover the contents of the vaults and accounts containing the proceeds from embezzlement and contract fraud. How can you be upset over that?"

"I'm," The Duke catches himself. The Prince smiles at both the King and Duke. Duke Yoritus drops his head, "We were investigating the same illegalities. You just beat us to the punch."

"Then you see father, we are working towards the same ends. Not together like you would like, but we are working towards the same goals." The Prince points out. "I am most sorry for beating you to it."

"Yeah, whatever, we have a battle to plan."

"Marckolius," His father starts, "You have been assigned a three ship strike force. The attack is to take place in three months, plenty of time for you and your friends to shape up your strike force to attack the Horde."

'*Tarapine* . . .' The Prince hears in his mind.

"We are taking on the pirates?"

"No, the Horde," Duke Yoritus corrects the Prince.

"The Horde is mostly made up of the Mezstarans," the Prince reminds them. "Are we attacking Tarapine?"

"In the morning you will take command of the strike force. We will send you the plans for the attack a few weeks before. Your job will be to follow your part of the plan for our coordinated attack."

"Of course Uncle Yori, what else would I do?"

"You will do exactly as you are commanded! This is not a joke or a chance to party with your friends. Lives will be on the line."

"I'm just pondering what trash heaps you are assigning to me!" The Prince responds.

"The ships are functional but they do need some shaping up. The crews are fresh from the academy. This is their mandated graduation tour, just as it is yours." The King leans over to the Prince, "You delayed graduating early to do this so here you have it. Enjoy your first command." The King hands a dark orange crystal to his son.

"I'll review this later." The Prince heads to the elevator.

"Take care of those trash heaps; they're all you're going to get!" The Duke taunts.

The Prince winks at his uncle as the elevator doors close.

Sitting around a large screen console in the Palace, the Prince, Viktorlo, and Brianto look over the contents of the dark orange crystal.

"Those ships are old, I mean really old!" Brianto looks upon the ship information with disbelief.

"I think calling them trash heaps is insulting a real trash heap." Viktorlo falls back in his chair.

"Guys, this is a test. We need to look at this with a positive attitude, an opportunity for us to get these ships back up and running. We don't need everything to work on these ships. We need propulsion, shields, and weapons. We need the power generation cores replaced and a complete refurbishment of the power systems."

"What about life support?" Brianto points out. "We are going to need to breath and be warm enough not to turn to space-cicles."

"Only on the decks we need it on. Strip the decks that we don't need, such as the crews quarters on two of the ships. We could use the third ship for the crew's quarters," Viktorlo says. "We could also switch out all of the energy weapons with missile launchers that use far less energy."

"All of these are great ideas. Let's figure this out tonight. We meet the command crews in the morning. Brianto, contact the Syndicate for use of their shipyards near Desespero. We might also be able to hire them to help."

"What do you want me to do?"

"Viktorlo, check on parts for your ideas, even old junk versions of these ships that we might be able to strip for parts. I'll have dinner brought up from the kitchens."

In the morning, they meet with two of the three captains of the ships. The captains explain the history of the ships, including combat experience.

"Stop," The Prince begins, "where is the other captain?"

"You didn't know? He is retiring from the service. We both are just a few months away from retirement ourselves."

The Prince smiles at them both. "Do you have it in you for one more mission?" They both answer yes. "Good, then let's have a tour of one of the ships. The crews from the academy will be here tomorrow."

"Will you be replacing the retiring captain?"

"I doubt it. Let's look at the crew assignments and the condition of the ships first." The Prince starts walking to the ships.

With the help of the two captains, the Prince works out the crew assignments and picks his command ship. They draw up the plans to revamp the ships.

"We've got an issue with the use of the Syndicate's shipyards." Brianto kneels down next to where the Prince is lying underneath a command console on the bridge.

"I'm trying to get this console working. What went wrong with our idea?"

"Apparently they are all booked up with refurbishing the primary strike force. Also, there doesn't seem to be any parts available or even old clunkers we could strip clean."

The Prince slides out from underneath the console. "I'll contact Anna about the parts or anything she might be able to scrounge up for us." The Prince pulls Brianto closer to him, "Contact the Lord General for use of the old shipyards there."

"You want to bring these ships to Gregoria?" Brianto forcibly whispers.

"Do you have a better idea? We need a shipyard to refurbish these trash heaps."

"These trash heaps are beyond rehab. They need to be stripped and sold off for parts."

"When all you have is a trash heap, you use that trash heap to the fullest. Now please go and make the arrangements. Let me figure out how to get these ships there without anyone noticing and get the parts we need."

"Fine, just remember to cut the transponders." Brianto suggests as he gets up and leaves the bridge.

The Prince gets up and enters a secluded communications room. He plugs his blue crystal into the communications console. The encrypted communications bridge is setup.

"I need to speak with Anna," Prince Marckolius states before the operator has a chance to ask whom he needs to speak within the Syndicate.

"My lovely Prince," Anna begins, "What may I do for you or with you."

"I get that my uncle decided to book up all of the available space at your shipyards and our shipyards can't do what we need done. But, you can't get the parts we need?"

"Not openly. You tell me where to have what you need delivered and I will deliver it personally." She smiles at him allowing her fangs to show. "Just tell me, how did you get stuck with that set of trash heaps?"

"My uncle thought it was a great way to get even with me. After all, he cannot complain to my father that I raided the vaults he shared with Osserate and the Ambassador, especially those two secret vaults of his. My payment, a set of trash heaps that should be recycled for parts and metal."

"You are funny. Just let me know when you get to where ever. I will have my men start to gather the parts you need."

"See you in about a week."

"I do hope so . . ."

A beep from the door catches the Prince's attention. "Yes?"

The door opens to both Brianto and Viktorlo standing there. "You are not going to believe this but only half of the shipyard is currently functional or accessible." Brianto tries to explain. "Something about bees or bez or something of the sort?"

"Beztra?"

"Yeah that's it. The Beztra have overrun part of the shipyard."

"This is what happens when you leave something unused for a very long time, things move in and won't leave on their own." The Prince lets out a long sigh. "I guess I am going to have to talk with the queen."

"They're bees; all they do is buzz around. If you get too close they will kill you." Viktorlo interjects. "Anyways, how are you going to communicate with them?"

"Face to face with the queen of the hive," the Prince stands up and walks out between them. "I will go and take care of this. Get these heaps ready to go. We will have to do short jumps until the hulls are resealed."

"Propulsion is ready on all three ships." Viktorlo hands a digital pad to the Prince.

"Then let's get a moving."

After a day of Interdimensional jumps, they arrive at the shipyard near Gregoria. The long concourse of the shipyard looks like a spine with no body. The half-lit shipyard shows no ships docked, the place is abandoned. Gregoria glimmers in the far distance showing only a blue and brown marble coloring with white blotches.

The ships dock allowing the Prince to disembark without much notice. He walks and walks until he reaches the sealed entrance to the Beztra inhabited portion of the shipyard. There are only dim emergency lights lit. He hears loud buzzing in the distance. The shipyard is in major disrepair.

As he walks into the hive area, he sees both adolescent and adult Beztra looking weak and frail. Their fur is dull. He walks through them, picking up vibes of starvation and fear. He walks until he reaches a large storage area with guards standing on each side of the door. They point their pikes at him and buzz their wings until they are almost off the ground.

"I am here to make your queen a proposition." The Prince says calmly. He waits for some kind of confirmation that they understand him. A long wait it seems until the doors slide open.

The guards step aside allowing him to pass. Honeycombs cover the walls of the dimly lit storage room. The queen stands from sitting at the far end in a large oversized honeycomb chair. She moves forward slowly to greet the Prince, buzzing softly as she moves.

"I am Prince Marckolius." The Prince bows slightly. "I am here to negotiate a way we can both use this facility. I noticed your children are starving. I can help if you let me."

"Prinze? Prinze of what?"

"I am hesitant to say because you will automatically think me to be evil. If I tell you I am a Warrior Priest, you will think I am a liar or an untrustworthy Gregorian. See my dilemma?"

"I will think neither. You are who you are. What iz thiz arrangement you zpeak of?"

"If I supply you with the nectars and foods you need for your hive may we use the shipyard to refurbish our ships?"

The queen sits on her hindquarters and scratches her beak. She looks at the Prince for a short while, "You can do thiz for uz?"

"I can and would."

"If you do thiz we will alzo help you with your zhip repairz. My children are great builderz and fazt flyerz. We can hold our breath for dayz in zpaze."

"What experience do your children have dealing with sealing the hulls of ships and other hull work?"

"We have generazional knowledge. We were onze great zhip builderz. We can zertainly handle thoze thingz you have out there. Why would a Prinze have zuch vezzles?"

"My payment, trash heaps for taking care of some unsavory business issues." The Prince looks mildly depressed.

"Well then, it iz agreed."

The Prince outstretches his hand and the queen taps it with one of her antennae.

CHAPTER 8

OUR MISSION

THE CLOUDS SWIRL ABOVE THE gate in the Great Temple on Gregoria. The loud cracks of thunder cause the Great Temple to shake as the white marble obelisks glow with white energy. In the blink of an eye, a pillar of white energy shoots down from the swirling clouds. The clouds dissipate above at the same rate the energy dissipates in the Great Temple.

Prince Marckolius stands in the center dressed in a white uniform with a dark blue sash. He rips the sash off and stomps it. He starts to leave the Great Temple when a glowing pair of eyes to his right catches his attention.

"You do know that your anger can adversely affect the gate and your transition?" A soft voice comes from the direction of the glowing eyes.

The Prince stops and turns to face the glowing eyes. "If I was you I would stay clear of Viktorlo. He is quite libel to chop you up into little bits."

The figure moves forward to show a fair skin biodroid wearing simple brown robes. It stops a few meters from the Prince.

"Good afternoon Prince Marckolius. Let me introduce myself," The biodroid puts out its right hand. "I am Kismet."

The Prince stares intently at Kismet, "You have a soul. That means you're from Cerebria."

"Very perceptive my young friend," Kismet continues to leave his hand outstretched.

'You can trust him,' echoes in the Prince's mind.

The Prince grasps his hand and pulls him closer, "You're the new Ambassador from Cerebria."

"I am the old Ambassador. I have been away a very long time. I came with a message to give you but only in private." Kismet is barely audible.

"This way, I don't have much time. I need to get back to the strike force to leave for the attack."

They leave the Great Temple and head into a confessional. The Prince seals the door and activates the privacy shield.

"Alright Kismet, we are now alone."

"I have a message from the Great Spark, our democratically elected leader. When you are ready, we are available to help you." The Prince looks blankly at Kismet. "Oh my, you haven't found yourself yet." A look of embarrassment spreads across Kismet's biodroid face. "I am really sorry. I thought . . . ." Kismet's voice drifts off. "I was thinking you were ready but it's too soon. I am sorry." Kismet bows slightly to the Prince.

The Prince stops him from leaving. "I have a few questions." Kismet steps back and looks inquisitively at the Prince. "What do you mean by too soon?"

"You are familiar with the prophesy?" The Prince shakes his head no. "The prophesy about you!"

"I am just the Crown Prince of the Proprietorship."

"You are a Destroyer. The most powerful one I have ever seen. However, you are more than just a Destroyer. You just haven't realized it yet," Kismet tries to explain. "But there is more than that. My question to you is this; do you fully understand all that information spinning in your head?"

"What does that have to do with anything?"

"The reason you do not understand all of the information is because you cannot put it into proper context until you realize who you are."

The Prince steps back and shakes his head. "I don't know who I am? I am a warrior."

"You got it confused. I can see who you are but telling you would do you no good. This is something you must figure out for yourself. You are not just a warrior. What you are is a Destroyer. That answers the what," Kismet taps the Prince on his chest directly over his heart. "This is where you will find yourself. This is where you will answer the question of who you are."

Silence stands between them for a moment.

"How old was your mother when she gave birth to you?" The Prince's expression changes to an even more confusing glare. "Just answer the question."

"She was 22 years of age. Why?"

"She wasn't 22 years of age. She had already gone through two rejuvenation cycles. She was about 200 years old, maybe more. How do you think she garnered all that information spinning in your head right now? I was there. I helped with the ancient transference device. You might not remember me because I wasn't using this particular biodroid model."

Disbelief shoots across the Prince's face. "This is nonsense. Why would she have lied about her age?"

"When you come out of the being rejuvenated you are 21 years old. You are normally sterile but your mother was not a normal woman. During her first life, she was a warrior priest. During her second life, she went on special missions and studied everything she could get her hands on, especially forbidden texts. That's why you have all that nonsense in your head right now. Once you find yourself all will be put into proper context." A loud banging occurs at the door to the confessional. "There is more but alas our time is up."

The Prince turns off the privacy shield and opens the door. Standing before the Prince is his grandfather.

"I heard Kismet was in the Great Temple waiting for you to return from Propri." His grandfather walks into the confessional. "Kismet, you did not clear having contact outside of the standard governmental circle."

"Pardon great Gregorian Larch." Kismet bows slightly, "I only wanted to pass along greetings from Cerebria to the Prince."

"How old was my mother when she gave birth to me?" The Prince questions his grandfather.

"I wonder who put that question into your mind?" he turns to Kismet, "You were told!"

Prince Marckolius gets in front of his grandfather to look him square in his eyes. "Please answer my question."

After a long pause, "201!"

"Then it is all true?" The Prince steps back and sit in a corner chair.

The Gregorian Larch sits next to him, "You must understand your mother was a very special woman. She figured out how to get around the sterility and have you."

"How much more don't I know?"

Kismet silently eases himself out of the confessional without notice. The Prince's grandfather clutches his hand. In a flash of light, they find themselves standing alone.

"Now then, you have questions?"

"I have one question that no one has ever been able to answer for me. Why did my mother leave that night to go and see Anna on Desespero?"

"You are old enough now to be able to comprehend what I tell you. When your mother was within her first life cycle, she married and had a daughter. That daughter went missing after here first rejuvenation. She tried to look for her ever since."

"How did she disappear?"

"No one knows for sure. Your sister was investigating something called the Bolder Gate. We have no idea of its location. It is rumored that the Bolder Gate is the entrance to Koasia."

"You mean to tell me my mother was married, had a daughter, and continued to look for her all the while marrying my father and becoming queen?"

"Her first husband died in a horrible accident near the Asmore Line, beyond the outer edge of the Andromeda Galaxy."

"So I have a half-sister? What about all of her missions?"

"Many are classified. When you mature all that information will come to you like a bolt of lightning from above. Your mother violated so many rules doing what she did to you. That device was forbidden! What is worse is your aunt and Kismet both assisted. It is due to that device you lost your sense of fear."

"Was anything ever found out about my half-sister?"

"I don't really know. You mother stopped filing reports before her second rejuvenation. Her secret mission was even a secret from me. You mother kept many secrets. You may want to have a conversation with your aunt at some point. Until then . . ." His grandfather lets go of his hand. "Stop by when you're done with your mission."

"Oh, I will see you when I get back."

The Prince walks onto the bridge deck of the strike force command ship. Viktorlo, Brianto, and both captains are there. He walks up to the holographic board in the back of the bridge and places a small orange crystal into the activation panel.

"We are to commence the attack tomorrow evening. We are to attack at 1800 hours on the dot. At 1805 hours my uncle's strike force should exit ID Space getting the drop on the pirates."

The Prince activates the holographic board. The board shows sixteen medium to large ships of various designs. All of them look ragged and in need of repair.

Viktorlo shakes his head, "If they are late we are dead!"

Both captains talk amongst themselves briefly. "I take it that your experience is telling you something?" The Prince interrupts.

"We cannot help but notice Sir that you did not configure these ships to follow the plan as shown."

"No, we figured that this was most likely a setup from the very beginning." The Prince looks at both captains. "I did not tell my father and uncle what our plans are in order to prevent my uncle from finding out what we are really going to do."

The Prince pulls the orange crystal and replaces it with a small brown crystal. The board shows the sixteen ships plus a very large luxury liner. The sixteen ships no longer look to be in disrepair.

"That large ship is the Galaxea. It was supposed to be lost years ago. It is being used as the pirates' command ship. Before you ask where I got this intelligence information, I got it from an alternate source through the Syndicate. Our regular intel has been scrubbed or falsified for some reason."

"Oh please," Brianto harrumphs. "You uncle is out to get us killed because he's now penniless!"

Viktorlo elbows Brianto in the ribs.

"We didn't sign on to die because of some family feud."

The Prince looks at both captains very seriously, "If you both do this then retire I will make sure you and your families will be well taken care of."

"We would not abandon you Sir."

"But thank you just the same."

"Alright, we will attack but in a different way and not at 1800 hours. We are going to wait and see if my uncle arrives on time. My overall plan is to take the Galaxea and the pirate command hierarchy." The Prince gestures to Viktorlo to continue the briefing.

"Pay attention to this," He begins. "The gutted ship is the slaved decoy. It is loaded up with missile launchers and rotary canons. They are old but effective. We will be following it out of ID Space behind the Tarapine sun. That will shield us from detection. We will follow the slaved decoy in single file so it will look like one single solar flare or wave from the sun. We will also pick up great momentum as we do this, effectively doubling our speed."

"We are using the sun's gravity to sling shot us into the center of this fleet?" One of the captains' asks.

"Yes, and that is just the beginning. Once we are on our way from the sun to the fleet the slaved decoy will be set loose. It will start firing everything it has as it goes into the center of the fleet. There it will remain launching all of its ammunition. Once the ammunition is depleted, it will automatically self-destruct inflicting even more damage to the pirate fleet.

"We will move side by side and ram the Galaxea on its broadside. The grapplers will engage allowing us to blow the port docs and board the Galaxea. The energy dampeners should kick in preventing energy weapons from use. It will be hand-to-hand combat. The Prince will lead the group from this ship and I will lead the group aboard from the other. The Prince will head to the bridge and I will head to engineering and auxiliary control."

"Brianto will stay aboard this bridge to make sure everything goes as planned." The Prince places his hand on Brianto's shoulder. "Are there any questions?" Both captains shake their heads no. "Good, then let's get moving. It's a day's travel with these old engines."

A cone vortex forms very near to the Tarapine sun. Bluish lightening erupts inside the vortex as each ship exits ID Space. The first ship looks dark and burnt all over its hull with missile turrets mounted every couple of meters. The next two ships look much cleaner and less armed. The three ships remain single file as they pass through the sun's corona, skimming the chromospheres. The shields of all three ships light up making the three ships look like one long solar flare emanating from the sun. Particles from the sun's corona continue to trail with the three ships as they break the sun's gravity.

"We are at 1805 my Prince," Brianto exclaims through the intercom. "No sign of the Duke's fleet."

"Have they detected us yet?"

"No sign of them turning towards us, we are nearing the first planet of the solar system. We still have several minutes to go before we are in full sensor range. It does look like the pirate ships are facing the direction we were supposed to exit ID Space from." Brianto strains to see the magnification of the visual sensors. Several of the cadets confirm.

"Then we were being setup all along," the Prince comments.

"We are sending the slaved decoy into the fray right now." Brianto hits the activation button on his console releasing the decoy ship from the navigation controls aboard the command ship. "It is moving away. Boy, are they in for a shock!"

"Prepare for impact in ten seconds!" The captain announces.

"The ships are now side by side. Brace yourselves down there." Brianto suggests.

"Five, four, ready, steady . . . ."

Through the missile strikes both ships impact the port side of the Galaxea. With the shattering of the shields, both ships drill dozens of meters in.

"The grappling arms have deployed." Brianto hits a series of buttons on his console. "I am blowing the air docks right now."

With a series of small explosions from each ship inside the Galaxea, armed men start to stream in. The damage internally to the Galaxea looks significant with buckling deck plates and collapsed blast doors. Sirens continue to go off with flashing red lights throughout the ship.

"What about the dampening field?" The Prince yells into a hand held communicator.

"It must have been damaged during the penetration of the ships. It won't activate," comes Brianto's response.

"Just get down here then. Grab as many of the crew that are left. I am heading to the bridge."

"Hey, leave a few for me."

"Brianto, the sooner you get down here the better chance you will get some. Now move it!" The Prince clicks off the communicator. "All of you follow me. Have those guns set to immobilize. We want plenty left for questioning." The Prince commands as his men follow him toward the stairs to go up.

As they move up through the ship, they only receive light resistance. They enter the shops area where all of the looted storefronts have jagged glass everywhere. There are bloodstains and scorch marks from gunfire but no bodies.

They climb another set of beautifully plush stairs to the lido deck. They move towards the front of the ship when the pirates start firing on them. The pirates are using the drained pool as a trench.

"Set up the mobile mortar cannons. We need to blow them out of that pool."

"Yes Sir." The men setup small portable mortar cannons.

The mortars launch at low angles and land inside the pool. The explosions rumble through the deck area. The men move forward with the Prince. Several more men run down the stairs that lead to the bridge only to explode as the Prince cuts them down with his sword.

"Be careful, the stairs are covered in their blood," whispers the Prince to the men following him. They see the red hue pulsing from his eyes.

They hear additional explosions from the lower bowls of the ship. The Prince and his men climb the stairs to the bridge. The Prince exits the stairs to see the pirate bridge crew all dead, their consoles blown out, and smoking. A single man in black leather stands at the front of the bridge, looking out into space.

"Well played Prince Marckolius." The man starts in a very raspy voice. He turns to the Prince showing a bomb vest with the switch in his right hand. His grayish beard and hair look well trimmed. "I cannot allow you to take me as the prize."

"I don't even know who you are." The Prince inches forward. "This is over and done, just surrender and the fighting ends." The Prince looks past the man to see most of the ships leaving into Interdimensional Space. Their vortexes dissipate quickly once they are gone.

"I was known as the Pirate King until this happened. Being completely caught off guard like this and the amount of damage caused by that missile barge of yours, the rest of the pirate captains voted a new leader and left."

"A name would be nice." The Prince continues to inch forward.

"My name is . . ." The Pirate King stops all movement. He stares forward at the Prince.

"You won't be needing this," The Prince takes the trigger out of the man's hand. "Men, check with Viktorlo for a status and turn off the alarms." The Prince pulls the vest off him and hands it to one of his men. "Please dispose of this safely."

"Yes Sir." The man bows and leaves with the vest.

The alarms stop as the Prince examines the Pirate King. "I have a feeling you have already purged this ship's computer but you cannot purge your mind." The Prince pokes the Pirate King's forehead with a finger. "You and I are going become very close here in a moment. Just so you know if you are who you say you are my men and I are in line for a very nice payday."

"Sir, Viktorlo reports that they have taken engineering and auxiliary command. The ship is ours!" The men bust out into jubilant celebration.

"We still have to get home. Contact Propri and request they bring ships to tow us. Additionally, report that we have taken the Galaxea and billions in booty from the pirates. That will motivate them to get here quickly." The Prince cracks a slight smile as he stares deep into the Pirate King's fearful eyes, "Include the fact that we have captured the former Pirate King, alive!"

The Prince places his hand on the former Pirate King's shoulder. He looks into his eyes and smiles. "Let's see what you really know. I have a few questions and you are going to answer them, truthfully."

The former Pirate King remains immobile. "Apparently I have no choice so ask away. I know very little."

"Why was this fleet pointing all of its weapons in the direction it was?"

"We received intelligence information that a strike force would attack us from that direction."

"Who provided the information?"

"Someone deep inside your uncle's command, I don't know who. The one that would have known was sitting at the far console when it exploded. You can die and ask him yourself."

The Prince looks to the back of the bridge to see Viktorlo coming up with Brianto. "How did it go down below?"

"Engineering is a mess. Most of the systems are booby-trapped. We deactivated propulsion, removed the booby traps from the cores, and sealed engineering." Viktorlo explains.

"That reminds me of something," The Prince turns back to the former Pirate King. "What happened to the original crew and passengers of the Galaxea?"

"Most of the original crew joined us, except for the captain and some officers. The passengers were a different story. We forced the men to join us. Any that fought us were killed with the captain and officers. The women were used and then sold off."

Disgust is apparent on most of those on the bridge, including the Prince. "What of the children?" The former Pirate King clamps his mouth closed trying to fight the urge to speak. A red hue returns to the Prince's eyes. "I order you to tell us what happened to the children?" The anger visible in his face, his mind transfixed on pulling every shred of information as he pulls the former Pirate King face to face with his. Their eyes locked together. "Adults are one thing you miserable wretch! Children are another, they are innocent."

"They were auctioned off to the highest bidder." Deep pain is present in his voice.

"The records, who were the bidders?" The question echoes.

"I don't know . . ." Tears start rolling down his face. "I don't know! They were taken to several slave worlds with the women. It's been over a year . . ." The Prince lets go allowing him to drop to his knees. "I don't know!"

Viktorlo runs up and grabs Prince Marckolius, "Stop! We need him alive."

The Prince stares down at him. "Your name is Aaron. What your men and you did is evil."

"I tried to do what I could! Please . . ." The former Pirate King stares up at the Prince with his hands clenched together, begging. He looks over at Viktorlo, "Cousin, please you have to believe me."

The Prince continues to probe his mind before letting go, "You are telling the truth." The Prince's eyes turn back to pure crystal blue. He looks at Viktorlo, releasing the former Pirate King. "Take him down to the brig where he belongs. Heavy guard, I don't want anything to happen to the former Pirate King. We will let the Proprietorship decide his fate. And Viktorlo, I already knew he was your cousin."

"A cousin far removed I assure you." Viktorlo grabs the former Pirate King by his shirt and removes him from the bridge.

CHAPTER 9

BANISHED!

Prince Marckolius enters the Proprietorship Boardroom. He straightens his white military uniform and jacket. Viktorlo and Brianto follow behind wearing off white military uniforms. All three wear various medals, decorations, and awards. The size and beauty of the boardroom rivals most ballrooms with inlaid gold and white marble walls. The onyx floor contrasts with the large gold chandeliers with elaborate crystals hanging above the 10,000-year-old dark granite boardroom table, at the end of which is an elaborate chair for his father, King Votcher.

Pairs of Royal Guardsman are at each door. Well-dressed men mill around the boardroom table discussing the latest politics and economic issues. Some shake the Prince's hand and pat him on the back.

"Marckolius," Viktorlo leans into the Prince, "I have that feeling. Something is wrong."

Prince Marckolius briefly stops shaking hands, "Take your place in the back with Brianto, and be ready."

Duke Yoritus enters the room causing all to go quiet. He raises his hands and then lowers them. "I am proud to introduce to my fellow Proprietors and special guests, my brother, King Votcher."

Everyone stands clapping as King Votcher enters the boardroom. He greets the Proprietors before sitting in his chair. "You may proceed."

The Duke bows to his brother before turning to face everyone. "I am happy to introduce to all of you, after a very long wait, my nephew and Crown Prince, Prince Marckolius."

The Prince stands to acknowledge their applause.

One of the older Proprietors stands, "I would like to read the proclamation."

Duke Yoritus interrupts, "I am sorry but many of the other Proprietors have requested official business be done first. Please pardon this change in the agenda." The Proprietor sits down with a bewildered look. "The business at hand refers to the recent accounting as disputed by several Proprietors."

The King taps Duke Yoritus on the shoulder. They confer privately for a moment before Duke Yoritus continues, "The recent influx of funds from the retrieval of confiscated accounts and vaults have been disputed by several Proprietors and their families. The retrieval process did not take into account prepaid contracts and additional funds from contract profits that were to be distributed to the rightful Proprietors here today."

An elderly Proprietor stands, "My Duke, shouldn't this be handled by the accountants, auditors, and lawyers?"

A brief amount of chatter occurs around the table. The Duke raises his hands quieting the group.

"Many of the Proprietors met with me, at some length, prior to our meeting here today. They express deep outrage at being deprived of their rightful moneys. Their numbers equal a quorum of the board here today. Those originally involved were briefed. A tablet with the specific charges and issues is being passed around now." Officers hand each Proprietor a digital tablet. "We will pause for a few minutes while each of you reviews the information."

The Prince looks around the table. Most of the Proprietors finish reading the information and look at the Prince with disdain and fear. The feeling towards the Prince changes drastically.

'They are about to twist the truth.' Warning echoes through the Prince's head.

"I have a couple of questions for the Crown Prince." Duke Yoritus glares at the Prince. "Please tell us why you recently confiscated those accounts?"

"Why do I feel like this is an inquisition?" The Prince mumbles to himself. "Your question is why I followed the letter of the law in confiscating the documented accounts containing the funds from fraudulent contracts, embezzled funds from contract mismanagement, and outright theft? Was I not supposed to follow the letter of the law and do my duty?" The Prince gazes around the boardroom table.

"It's not so much what you did but how you did it?" The Duke starts to explain, "What we are complaining about is your lack of utter thought in the way you systematically confiscated everything and anything having to do with your investigation. Your over aggressiveness has irreparably harmed many around this esteemed table and has caused them to lose all confidence in you."

"I did my duty to the letter of the law. It is not my duty to figure out where the money came from. That's what the accountants and auditors are for."

The Duke looks at several of the Proprietors. They bow their heads to him, "Until this issue is resolved you and your friends are to return all funds awarded to you for the recovery of these accounts. You are also stripped of your title as Crown Prince and the authority that came with that title, until further notice."

The Prince looks at his father, "Are you going to allow this?"

The King stands, "I request a vote on this. The rules state there must be a two thirds majority, not just a quorum."

"Very well brother," The Duke motions to all around the table, "I ask each of you to raise your hand if you support the disciplinary action against the Prince and his friends." All but a few raise their hands. "The motion carries for the discipline of the Prince and his friends. Let the records show this."

The Prince's father motions for him to come forward. "I am sorry but you know that the Proprietorship has spoken," whispers the King. "There is nothing I can do."

The Prince looks with disbelief, "Uncle Yori and the rest of them are upset because a lot of what we recovered was theirs. I don't know what type of illegal dealings he's up to with them but . . ."

"I will not stand for conspiracies. You might never have the authority, even when I die. It isn't up to me anymore. It's up to them. They will most likely change the succession to the crown because of this if you don't beg them for leniency."

"Fracken' Bull! This is all bull!" The Prince storms away from his father.

The King looks upset as the Duke starts again, "You are hereby stripped of the title and authority of Crown Prince by orders of the Proprietorship."

"I heard you the first time." The Prince's eyes begin to develop a red hue. "So I am being punished for doing my duty? Is that right father?" The Prince hits the table with his fist causing the table to chip.

The Duke smiles broadly, "All of your accounts have been frozen, what few we found. We did the same with your friend's accounts. Such a shame this happened."

The Prince looks at his father, "You are going to let him get away with this just like he got away with having my mother murdered?"

The Duke runs around the table, pushing aside several Proprietors.

"You know the rules boy!" The Duke angrily looks into Prince's eyes. "You make an accusation you have to back it up with evidence."

"Are the cameras rolling in here?" The Prince looks at Viktorlo's father, the Captain of the Royal Guard. The response is a head bob of yes. "If you look under my work directory you will find a single encrypted file. You can unlock the file with the code 260327846778. You might like the contents my dearest uncle."

"Really?" The Duke takes a step back.

"Oh yes, the signed contract for the murder of my mother with your signature!' The Prince leans into his uncle and whispers, "Try getting out of that."

His uncle pulls his sword only to have the Prince pin it against the table with his own. All of the Proprietors and those in the back of the room hurry to the exits.

"Stop this nonsense!" Yells the King. "This is not going to solve anything. You two must stop this before you damage the boardroom."

"Shut up Votcher. And get out!" The red hue in the Duke's eyes causes the King to exit the room with his guards.

"I have something for you boy that you would never know!" The Duke taunts.

He steps back, holding his sword up to block the Prince's attack; the Duke smacks him in the face with the hilt of his sword. The Prince wipes a small amount of blood from the side of his mouth.

"Have you ever heard of a rich divorce boy? Good old fashioned traditional rich divorce."

"How dare you," the Prince charges at his uncle. "My father would never have my mother assassinated to get out of their marriage!"

The Duke thrusts back only to hit the boardroom table causing a large crack. He moves to the opposite side of the table and pulls out a small grenade.

"Your father had me help him with the divorce because he was too spineless to do it himself. Why do you think he helped cover up everything?" He pulls the pin and sets the grenade in the center of the table. "The cameras were never on today boy. Given that, let's see who they blame for this?" The Duke turns and starts running out the side door.

The Prince bolts to the rear exit.

He reaches his friends in the hall, "Go, go, go! He set a grenade to blow."

All three run as the grenade goes off. Debris flies out through the rear double doors of the boardroom, causing the large ornate brass doors to fall off their hinges hitting the floor with a reverberating thud. Pieces of the wall fall into the hallway. The shock causes the guards to fall to the floor as they run past them. The sirens blare with an ear-piercing screech.

"Where are we going?" Viktorlo catches up to the Prince.

"The only way we can escape without killing everyone, through the gate." The Prince leads the way into the palace.

They weave their way through the hallways as the alarms continue to screech, encountering light resistance along the way. Arriving at the gate room, they catch their breath.

"Did your uncle blow up the 10,000 year old granite symbol of the Proprietorship?" Viktorlo wipes some blood off his shirt.

"And, why did your father let all that happen?" Brianto hits a guard hiding behind one of the obelisks of the gate knocking him out.

"I don't really understand what happened or how it happened. What I do know is that we need to go before more guards come to their deaths."

"We didn't kill them all." Brianto drags the guard's body away from the gate.

"Just get in the circle." Prince Marckolius raises his arms. The clouds begin to swirl above the palace. Lightening crashes down. The white energy builds within the gate until a burst of it shoots upward into the swirling clouds.

A couple of days later on Gregoria, Prince Marckolius watches other Warrior Priests go through their training.

Viktorlo runs up to him, "Marckolius, your father wants to talk to you. We have been looking for you all over the place."

"Really, it's only been a little over two days!" The Prince grinds his teeth.

"Come on, your father's waiting. Maybe they have come to their senses." Viktorlo grabs the Prince's arm. "We knew you would be here or the temple. We checked the temple first."

They walk into a conference room in the training complex. Brianto moves to the far corner of the room. Viktorlo takes the other seat just outside of the video camera's range. Prince Marckolius taps the activation button on the control panel below a large display screen. The screen hums to life displaying his father.

"Marckolius, I hope all is well?" His father's long face and sunken eyes show deep disappointment.

"I am doing fine, given what happened."

"I want to explain to you . . . . I want to explain to you exactly what happened. The Proprietorship found that you were far too aggressive in fulfilling your duties. This brought about your removal as the Crown Prince. It may have taken years but you would have eventually regained their confidence and your title. Then the 10,000-year-old boardroom table was blown up. Not to mention the complete destruction of the boardroom."

"That was my uncle," Prince Marckolius starts, "He set off a grenade in the center of the table. You know I only carry my sword with me."

"Were the guards you and your friends killed on your way to escape also his fault?" A hint of anger comes out from Marckolius' father. "It doesn't matter. I wanted to tell you myself, you have been completely removed."

The Prince looks blankly at his father. "Removed?"

After a long pause, "You have been banished from the Proprietorship."

"Banished!?!" The Prince becomes livid. "Banished from the Proprietorship? I am your son. I am next in line to the throne!"

"Not anymore. Your stunt changed everything! The Proprietorship has ruled and I am powerless to change it."

"You mean I am no long a Prince?" Tears start from Marckolius' eyes.

"You can never return to Propri without being thrown into prison. Your friends, on the other hand, may return if they pay the fines, return their share of the confiscated money, and publically apologize."

Marckolius is speechless as he wipes away the tears. He shakes his head as if to clear it. He looks up at his father, "I will relay that to them. I have a question for you. At what point where you neutered?"

"Excuse me?"

"At what point did you become a figure head instead of the ruler? I guess I knew it deep down but I refused to admit it. The way you would cover for my uncle."

His father drops his eyes, "I am really sorry this happened. I wish it could have been different."

"It could have if you had stood up and defended me. You know as well as they know that I was only doing my duty!" Marckolius' anger starts to rise. "I stood up for you. I defended you. I helped defend the Proprietorship. I worked my tail off. My friends worked their tails off. And what do we get in return? How are we rewarded?"

"Marckolius . . . ."

"Just pray that they and I never cross paths because all that will be left is a blood trail!" Marckolius crushes the controls to the screen, disconnecting the call. He falls forward allowing his forehead to rest on the dark display screen. "I'm sorry for dragging you both through this. You heard my father, if you want to return I will cover the costs."

"I don't know about Viktorlo but I have no intentions of leaving. I do want to bring my mother here. She never liked the palace much anyways."

Marckolius pulls out a digital pad. He types for a moment before handing it to Brianto. "Go ahead, type in your account number here on Gregoria and hit enter."

"A million credits?"

"It will cover getting your mother here and setting her up comfortably." Marckolius turns to Viktorlo, "How about you?"

"I said it before and I will say it again, our destiny is intertwined with yours. I can't go back nor do I really want to."

"What about your father? He's still the Captain of the Royal Guard."

"He was asked to retire." Viktorlo looks away briefly. "He's decided to retire and move far away from Propri. Your Father is helping him."

"I'm so glad to hear that. Still, if they need anything . . ." Marckolius' voice drifts off.

"Why don't you go back to your condo and rest, we have lots to do. If I need any money I know where to get it." Viktorlo pats Marckolius on the back.

"Yeah, rest." Marckolius turns away, opens the door, and slowly walks out.

He climbs into the back of the limo only to find his aunt there.

"Get in. We need to chat." His aunt seems very stern.

Marckolius gets in. The driver closes the door after him.

"I heard," His aunt begins. "I'm sorry this happened."

"Don't be. I didn't belong there anyways." Marckolius wipes his eyes.

"I know. The intelligence community has been all abuzz about you being banished." She leans in and hugs Marckolius.

"Banished!"

"It will take some adjustment for you. Take some time and relax. It won't seem so bad in a few days."

"They banished me for doing my duty."

"I know." His aunt pulls him close and hugs him again.

"They banished me and my father was powerless to stop them, powerless to stop my uncle." Marckolius softly speaks. "That's what hurts the most. My father couldn't stop them and he's supposed to be the King. Aunt Marianus, my father went along with it. He did little to defend me. So now, I am banished!"

CHAPTER 10

FIRST THINGS FIRST

THE JUNGLE HEAT AND HEAVY rains cause a thick steamy fog. Visibility is near impossible as Marckolius moves through the jungle. Out of breath, he runs. Thick salty sweat pours down into his eyes blurring everything. Marckolius slips and then slides in mud flowing trenches. Down, down, down he reaches out and grabs a small tree. He barely holds on while dangling over the cliff seeing someone standing below. Someone, unknown, dressed in white robes standing below untouched by the heavy hot rains. The man strokes his short white beard.

'Are you coming or not. I'm not going to wait forever!' The old man yells upward.

'Who are you?'

The old man laughs loudly, 'Don't you need to figure that out for yourself?'

Marckolius springs straight up in bed drenched in sweat; his eyes wide open, panting. A hard rain pounds against the windows. After showering and dressing, Marckolius walks into his living room and sits on the long leather couch with a breakfast drink. He sits, staring out the large window watching the rains pour down over the city. He sips his drink from time to time sitting in the dark of the day.

The doorbell rings. He continues to sit, looking out as the rains continue. The doorbell rings over and over and over again. He continues to sit. The door clicks as it slides open.

"Do you plan on leaving this condo ever again?" His aunt walks in and closes the door.

He continues to look out at the pouring rain. His aunt sits down next to him, taking the glass from his hand, and placing it on the glass table nearby.

"Alright, you are coming with me. You have been cooped up in here for two weeks. Your sulking is over!" She pulls on his arm.

"I haven't been sulking." Marckolius says. "I have been praying and meditating."

"You're lost right now. It's time for you to find yourself. Now get up and get dressed so we can get going."

"You're not going to leave me alone are you?"

"Your sarcasm is unbecoming nephew. Now, get dressed!"

They enter the long black limo through a private area. The limo hovers above the ground. The limo exits into the heavy rain. The raindrops evaporate as they hit the windshield and windows. Traffic is very light. Marckolius continues to look out into the rain.

"You seem very distracted. What are you looking for out there?"

"We are being followed." The words come out softly with no emotion.

"Yes, your grandfather decided you needed extra protection, just in case."

"I already know about them." He points to the other side of the limo. "I mean the two others out there, most likely sent by my uncle."

"I see. Do you believe they are dangerous?"

"No, they're not assassins or part of the Duad Bantam. They are just spies. I may want to talk to them tonight, just to stay in practice."

"Harrumph! You might not care about yourself but we do care about you. Show some concern for your own wellbeing once in a while!"

The limo slows down and turns into the underground facility that is part of the Great Temple Complex. The limo stops in a private area. Both exit the limo and enter an elevator.

"Up to the temple," His aunt commands.

They exit to the long marble hallway leading to the rear entrance. His aunt walks briskly in front while Marckolius walks slowly with his head down.

"Coming?" She calls back to him as she reaches the large wooden ornate doors to the Great Temple.

Marckolius reaches the doors and pushes them open. His aunt follows him in. Candles dimly light the temple. They walk up to the large white marble obelisks.

"We are alone except for the six warrior priests guarding the temple." Marckolius points out.

"They are quite attentive now. When you met Kismet here, he was able to sneak in remaining silent until you arrived. All of the guards had to be retrained."

"They were bored guarding a gate that rarely gets used. I hardly blame them."

"Apathy now? You just keep lowering yourself down and down."

"No, realism. Now then, why are we here?"

"You were invited to meet someone a week or so ago. You have been ignoring the invitation. It's not polite to ignore meeting invitations." His aunt points out.

"You mean those nightmarish dreams I've been having? I don't take kindly to that."

"The person is very important and can help you immensely."

"What do you want me to do?"

"Sit down in the middle of the gate. Sit anyway you like but sit in the exact middle."

Marckolius sits down in the center of the gate, crossing his legs.

"Now, access the gate's network."

"If I'm going someplace should I not be standing?" His aunt shoots him a look of irritation. "I mean, really, you have to be standing in order to exit the gate at your destination point."

"You aren't going anywhere, at least not physically."

"Then why am I accessing the gate network?"

The irritation boils up, "Just do what I am telling you to do. Now close your eyes and access the gate's network." His aunt clenches her hand into a fist. "Are you accessing the gate's network?"

"Yes."

"Good, now look to your right. What do you see?"

"I see a green pulsing orb not connected to the network."

"Finally," The exasperation his aunt feels comes out. "Connect to it."

Marckolius opens his eyes and looks at his aunt. "You must be joking. This could be an assignation attempt or something. How do I know who I am supposed to be meeting?"

"Just connect to it before I belt you one. You have to be this obstinate?" She yells angrily at him with her voice reverberating back. "Connect to the green pulsing orb now!"

"Fine, but if this is an assignation attempt you're the one at fault." Marckolius feels a swat to the back of his head causing him to fall over.

"Your sarcasm is not appreciated." His aunt stands over him, pointing her right index finger between his eyes. "My tolerance is about at an end. You want help in figuring things out or not?"

"Alright, I will do it. Just get out of the gate circle." Marckolius reseats himself.

His aunt exits the gate to stand nearby, "Are you going to do it or not?"

"Maybe . . ."

The obelisks glow with a white energy. In a flash of brilliant white light Marckolius finds himself sitting on old sand stone fashioned into a circle. There is a light breeze with no discernible temperature. The sun above is almost blinding. There is sand everywhere.

"I'm in the middle of a desert?" Marckolius brushes sand off his pants as he stands.

"Not really." Marckolius turns to see the old white robed man from his dream. "It is about time, I was starting to think you were never going to accept my invitation."

Marckolius walks up to him, "Who are you?"

"I am a friend. You on the other hand cannot answer that same question."

"I meant your name?"

"Then that is what you should have asked. Answer the question of 'Who are you?' and I will tell you my name. Simple when you think about it. Come on, it is sometimes easier to talk and walk."

Marckolius reaches down and picks up a handful of sand. "This is texture. There's a certain consistency to the sand along with grit."

"It's just sand."

Marckolius looks at the old man. "This isn't sand. It can't be. This is something more."

"It's just beyond your reach, isn't it?"

Marckolius lets the sand fall from his hand. He watches it closely. "There is a slight breeze but the sand falls back to where I picked it up from."

"So young man, tell me, what is it you care about?" The old man turns to look Marckolius in his crystal blue eyes. "You have your mother's eyes."

"You knew my mother?"

"Only briefly," he strokes his short white beard. "Did you want to answer?"

"What I care about?" Marckolius shakes his head trying to think.

"Clear your mind and listen to your heart." The old man taps him on his chest.

"That's what Kismet told me."

"Interesting, those old Cerebria are very interesting indeed. He gave you some great rare advice. You haven't followed it yet. I might not have either, given the thought. Let's walk."

They walk and walk and walk. "Where are we going?"

"Do you know who you are yet?"

"No."

"Then we continue walking. The sand isn't bothering you yet, is it?"

"Why would it bother me? Is it bothering you?"

The old man has a look of impatience on his face. "Alright, you're not getting this. I have never before met anyone this dense. Admit what is in your heart and end the conflict in your head."

Marckolius stops. He takes a deep breath then lets out a long deep sigh. "I care about my friends. I care about those that are close to me. I care about those who I am responsible for." He turns to the old man. "I am to blame for so much. All I ever wanted to do was to protect my father and my friends from my uncle. Instead I really screwed things up."

"Did you now?" The old man strokes his beard. "You got them out of there, off Propri. You pulled off more than anyone expected. You even changed Gregoria forever."

"Not if my uncle comes after me. He wants it all back and that means he has to do something about me. I am still his greatest threat."

"So, you still think this is all about you? Your uncle is only interested in you? How arrogant!"

"It's not all about me. I have to protect them. I can't let my uncle come after Gregoria."

"How do you know he will come after you? How do you know he will come only after Gregoria? How do you know what he will do?"

"My uncle is driven by power and money. He will want to raid the vaults on Gregoria and the church." Marckolius looks deeply concerned. "If my uncle cuts them off from outside resources such as fuel like he did before they could start to collapse. Their allies are fearful, as my uncle has raided different planets, kingdoms, and other places. I am currently powerless to do anything."

"Have you heard anything you have told me?" The old man strokes his beard even more.

"I want to protect those I care about . . ." Marckolius pauses for a long while. "I'm a walking, talking, insane paradox."

The old man smiles broadly, "Do you know who you are now?"

"I'm a protector but I'm also a destroyer. How is that possible?"

The old man steps back as Marckolius' stops moving. Bluish energy spikes around him. In an instant, vapors lift off his skin. A few sparks spew from his mouth and nose. Everything blurs around them both. The sand gives way to stars. The bright sun dissipates. A light blue wavy grid appears as the floor. All around them are stars, planets, and galaxies.

"So, you tell me how that is possible." The old man grabs Marckolius' arm. "Do you know the answer to your question?"

"God!"

"Do you know the word, the one single word that can bring fear to anyone who hears it? Do you know the truth?"

Marckolius stares out, looking about himself in wonder and awe. "I know, I know."

"Do you know where you are now?"

"The Celestial Plenum," Marckolius answers without hesitation. "This is the legendary meeting place of the ancient gods. This is how they looked in on everyone."

"Do you know how to control your perspective?"

Marckolius puts forth his hand. Space shifts around them quickly to show Gregoria and her moon. Marckolius zooms in on the Great Temple.

"I can see myself with my aunt standing there."

"Good control. Now, do you know how to change universes?"

With waves of his hand, the universe changes around them with a flash of lightening. The blurring stops to show Propri. Marckolius puts forth his hand. In a blur, a large shipyard appears with ships of various classes in differing stages of repair. Marcolius zooms in on a larger ship.

"That's the Cerci, my uncle's command ship. They are building. They are preparing for something."

"Well now, I guess I should tell you my name."

"Ophion, your name is Ophion. You're a Galactic, one of the elders from the third civilization of man." Marcolius turns to Ophion to see surprise. "My mother knew far more about you and the Galactics than you thought. She read every single forbidden and obscure text she could get her hands on."

"How much can you access now?"

"All of it. Every shred of knowledge mother transferred to me when I was five years old. This was to keep me from becoming like my Proprietor ancestry, my dad, and uncle."

"I think she would be most impressed with you."

In an instant blur of harsh lightning, the universe disappears. A planet shows itself, surrounded by a space of flames. Winged things swoop over and around the planet. The figure in the distance sits on a throne of blood and howling souls.

"What are you doing? Return to our universe, quickly before he notices us!" The panic in the old man's voice causes Marcolius to switch back to the universe he is physically in. "What did you think you were doing?"

"I needed to know where the Earth is. My God, how?"

"You could have gotten us killed. Yes, there are places and persons capable of not just sensing us when we look in upon them, but they can do major harm to us. That was Hell and that was . . ."

"I now understand why everyone is so afraid of me. I could have become like my namesake, the First King, but far more powerful. It would have been so easy to take control of the Proprietorship. Everyone would know fear. It would have been so easy!"

Ophion pats Marcolius on the back, "But you didn't. You aren't like the First King. You aren't like them. You are you. And now you know what you must do."

"So, I'm supposed undo what the First destroyed? Wait, the Earth still exists so he couldn't have destroyed it. How do I get the Earth out of Hell?"

"First things first young man, you have to figure out how you're going to stop your uncle."

"I need to protect Gregoria. The only way I am going to do that is to use all of that money to build a war fleet and an alliance that can rival my uncle's."

"When you're done, seek out a kingdom worthy of your soul. Build it. Create it if you have to. Just don't look in on the Earth! That time will come one day."

Marckolius stares blankly for a moment, "First things first, I have to organize and build." He places his hand out, "I want to thank you."

Ophion takes his hand, "No, thank you young man. You and your friends give me hope for the future of all of us. You better get going."

Marckolius smiles, turns and fades out as he walks away.

Marckolius reaches out and stops his aunt's hand from swatting him again. "My dearest aunt, why do you feel the need to swat me?" Marckolius stands up.

"There was a slight flash from the obelisks but the time was too short for you to have left and come back. You need to sit back down and do it this time."

Marckolius pulls close to his aunt and whispers, "I just came from speaking with Ophion."

"That means . . ." His aunt hugs him, "What's next for you?"

"I need to get with Viktorlo and Brianto. My uncle will be eventually coming here. We have a lot of work to do if we are going protect Gregoria and what allies we have left. First things first, we need to build."

CHAPTER 11

THE REAL WORK IS ABOUT TO BEGIN!

MARCKOLIUS, VIKTORLO, AND BRIANTO STAND together at the training grounds for warrior priests. They all wear black leather pants, fore arm gauntlets, and black leather boots.

"I still can't believe we are going to do this." Brianto breaks the silence. "You got the Lord General to agree to the new training regime."

"We will see what the six best fighters have to say about this." Viktorlo nudges Marckolius, "You've been overly quiet as of late. Is everything alright?"

"I've just been thinking about what we need to be doing. We still need to figure out what my uncle is up to."

"Why don't we pay Propri a visit?" Brianto interjects.

"That's a good idea!"

"Marckolius that is not a good idea," Viktorlo scolds. "You do understand that if we return we will all be thrown into prison."

"Viktorlo," Marckolius pats him on his back, "You've got to figure Propri would be the last place they would ever think we would turn up. We would catch them by surprise."

"I was just trying to make a joke." Brianto tries to explain. "Don't take my suggestion seriously."

"That was a fantastic idea. You don't give yourself enough credit."

Viktorlo leans over to Brianto, "There's no talking him out of it. We are really screwed."

"No we are not. We can do it. We just need to plan our redirection and something else to go with it, but that's for another discussion."

Marckolius points to the six warriors that come out to the training yard. Marckolius steps forward, "If you would please line up."

"We were told to give up our vacation to come here for some new type of training? Exactly where are the trainers?"

"You are Terada? I have heard good things about you." Marckolius walks forward.

"I don't know who you are at all. None of us know who you three are." Terada and the others chuckle slightly.

All six bow as the Lord General approaches. Marckolius, Viktorlo, and Brianto bow slightly. The Lord General's long white robes sway only slightly as he moves. His long gray hair gives him an elderly look.

"Marckolius, my boy, I would like a word." The frail voice is barely audible.

Marckolius walks over to him, "Of course Lord General."

"I would like to make sure that you will not kill these unsuspecting warriors."

"I wouldn't kill them. Why would you think that?" Marckolius gives a defensive look.

"You have a history and a reputation with the upper ranks. You tend to be far too aggressive at times."

"I promise you that I will show restraint. None of them will be killed but injuries are not out of the question."

"I remember when you took down your trainers at the age of fourteen. One was forced to retire due to injuries." The Lord General shoots Brianto and Viktorlo a nasty look as they chuckle at the comment. "Well then, since I have your word, please start the training session."

Marckolius bows slightly as the Lord General moves to a seat under some shade. Marckolius moves forward to face the six warriors.

"My name is Marckolius. The others are Viktorlo and Brianto. You were asked here to learn critical new ways of combat so you can teach the new recruitment class."

"And what makes you so much better than us?" Terada walks forward to face Marckolius.

"I'll tell you what, you six figure out which of you is the best. I will face the best of you in unarmed combat."

"We already did that and it's me." Terada points to himself.

"Alright, then let's walk out into the training yard to start this." Marckolius begins walking out.

Terada walks to the center of the training yard. He bows and quickly jumps toward Marckolius. Marckolius counters, allowing him to go past and fall face first in the dirt.

"Is it normal for a distinguished warrior to attack before your opponent is ready?" Marckolius steps back away from Terada. "You can get up and brush yourself off anytime you like."

Terada gets up, brushing himself off while staring the entire time at Marckolius. They assume positions across from each other. Both bow slightly to each other. Marckolius slides to the right allowing Terada to go past him again. Terada spins trying to kick the feet out of Marckolius only to find he isn't there. He looks up to see Marckolius coming down on him. Terada braces himself but Marckolius only taps him on the top of his head before stepping back again.

"You didn't even try to block me. Why would you do that?" Marckolius blocks several strikes.

"You missed with your attack, didn't you?" Terada misses repeatedly. "Stand still!"

Terada's spin kick misses as Marckolius slides beneath taking his leg out. Terada again lands face first in the dirt. Marckolius plops on top of him and finds a comfortable seat.

"Are you done yet?" Marckolius has yet to break a sweat.

"Get off of me!"

Marckolius looks out to see the other five running towards them. He puts out his hand and they stop mid stride. Marckolius walks over to them. He looks each one in the eyes.

"You five are to watch and learn. Please sit where you are standing." Marckolius gestures for them to sit. He releases them after they sit straight down. "That is much better." Marckolius turns to walk back when Terada attacks him.

Marckolius blocks the attacks. Spin, drop, parry, over and over again. Terada's frustrations mount as beads of sweat pour from his brow. Marckolius allows Terada to step back to catch his breath.

The Lord General stands up, "If you both don't mind I have a meeting I must attend to shortly. How much longer will this continue?"

Terada attacks Marckolius with the same results again. This time Marckolius' open palm hits him in the stomach, windpipe, and then a shock thrust upwards to the chin. Terada goes airborne backwards.

'Catch him!' Marckolius hears in his mind.

Marckolius runs and slides between the five sitting warriors. He catches Terada, laying him gently on the ground. The shock on the faces of those sitting freezes them. Marckolius looks him over.

"Take deep breaths. You only got the wind knocked out of you. Your jaw is going to be sore for a day or two." Marckolius rubs his windpipe area and chest.

"I'll be fine." Terada whispers.

Marckolius looks at the five, "You never saw me run and slide? How many hits did I put on Terada just a minute ago?"

"Two" They all agree.

"No, three hits, one to the stomach, one to the windpipe, and then the thrust upward to the chin. You have to be able to see these things or you will all be dead. There are many races considerably faster than most of you. Vampires are a good example," Marckolius explains.

Marckolius stands and walks back to the Lord General.

"You did not have to end it right there if you didn't want to."

"No Lord General, I was trying to get him to react faster but it would seem he was already at his limit. Anymore and it would have been abusive." Marckolius grabs a white hand towel, wiping himself off.

"Well now, you certainly showed restraint. I ask you, can they be taught? Can they learn to stop someone like you?"

"No. We can teach them to stop vampires, Intican, and plenty of others. That is the idea behind this. We will instill a new curriculum into their training and what they train others. We will rebuild our forces. Just remember though, the new recruits will have a mix of races. I am hoping that will help."

"You are ambitious. I wish you lots of Devine Intervention. You might need it." The Lord General walks into the training complex.

Viktorlo hands each of the six digital pads. "These pads contain new fighting strategies. Study them tonight. Be back here at 1300 hours this afternoon. Be warmed up and ready go. You will be put through your paces so we can measure your current physical endurance limits."

Marckolius, Viktorlo, and Brianto walk into a secluded area within the training complex.

"I have every intention of going back to Propri this Sunday, if possible."

"Marckolius, that's insane. What are we going after?" Brianto sits in a corner chair.

"As I said before, we have to have a diversion. We just can't use the gate either." Viktorlo sits down.

"I have an idea that I thought about doing years ago. How about if I retrieve my mother's casket and body for a proper burial here on Gregoria?"

"I have never heard of taking a dead body through the gate. Maybe you should hire a transport to bring your mother's body back here. You would really have to trust them though." Viktorlo ponders, "We may need something more than just that. I figure we can take care of some final items like family business."

"You two will get into the system and retrieve my uncle's proposals and plans to the Proprietorship. Secondly, try to get a copy of the latest version of the communication codes. I will have my mother's body dug up and loaded onto the transport. I will then go and see my father, maybe for the last time."

Brianto asks, "What do you plan to accomplish by seeing your father?"

"It will give the total diversion necessary for you two to complete your mission. I will be the focus, not you. I will get their attention. Of course, we will also use the gate to escape back to here." Marckolius sits down.

"That would definitely grab your uncle's attention." Viktorlo leans in, "We will need to borrow that magic blue crystal of yours."

"I will contact Kismet to have a copy of it made. You aren't going to get the original."

"What is so damn significant about that crystal?" Brianto asks.

"My mother left it for me here on Gregoria. The instructions said it would unlock every door, activate any computer, override almost all command codes, and allow me to move about the Proprietorship without notice. It has worked quite well for us."

"Who do you plan on asking for help with the transportation?"

"Anna," Viktorlo closes his eyes and falls back in his chair to Marckolius' answer. "If you have a better idea, then let's hear it."

"Nope, just checking on my suspicions of Anna and you, that's all."

"Do you think she will send Telibina?"

"Alright Brianto, contact her and setup the transportation to there and the transportation of a casket with body, intact, back to Gregoria."

"Do not encourage him." Viktorlo scolds. "You know what he's going to do."

"Yeah, I'm going to setup the transportation. I was wondering how I should pay the Syndicate."

"Half before and the other half upon delivery," Marckolius walks out of the room.

"You keep it clean. Don't be using this as an excuse to meet up with her."

"Viktorlo, you pay attention to the training and I will take care of this."

Marckolius walks out into the training yard alone. He looks around the area.

'You should leave,' echoes in his mind.

A darkish figure walks out from behind a couple of bushes. The smell of crimson fills the air. Ash floats off the figure as the wind lightly blows.

"And what would bring something like you out of your pit?" Marckolius starts stretching.

"And you thought I hadn't noticed you? Not many have ever peered into my realm before." The dark figure walks up to Marckolius.

"I was only trying to figure out where in the Multiverse the Earth had been phased to."

"You weren't planning on trying to steal my prize, were you?"

"No, I have plenty of other things to do. Anyways, I wouldn't even begin to know how."

The dark figure laughs slightly, "A fine sense of humor. I was wondering, why are you futzing around this place when you could have taken the Proprietorship? You could easily take it all. If you need any help, well I would be more than happy to assist. After all, Destroyers tend to lean to me."

"That's OK, I get plenty of help. Anyways, the Proprietorship is far too corrupt for me to rule over it without killing off almost the entire ruling class. It's not worth the time and effort."

"Hmmmm, you may have a point. Well, I have been meaning to thank you for all of those souls you have dispatched my way. Some of them have been most delectable."

"I'm glad you liked them. I am sure there will be plenty more to come."

"Oh yeah, I am most certain of that. Destroyers traditionally keep their Angels of Death quite busy. Yours is sort of cowering off to the side of you right now. What type of Guardian Angel cowers like that?"

"Thank you for your concern." Marckolius stops stretching to look into the black ash soot eyes of the dark figure. "Obviously you have something to say so just say it so you can go off and cause havoc elsewhere."

"Fine, I can give you anything you want. Any kingdom you want. I can make your life plush and easy. I can deliver all your enemies to your feet, including your uncle. All you have to do is prostrate yourself to me." Marckolius openly chuckles. "Well, I had to ask. It is what I do."

"Yeah, it's what you do."

"I would ask you to stay out of my realm, though." The dark figure's demeanor changes to a very serious fiery look. "The next time you show up I will kill you and take your soul. You got that?"

"Yep, got it, stay out or you will kill me, exactly what I suspected."

"Just don't, no matter how tempting it is, unless I tempt you."

"You are confused. Must be senility brought on by your age."

The dark figure smiles broadly to show dark yellowish fangs. "I'm not joking. Stay out!"

"One day we will have to meet on the Elysian Fields between Heaven and Hell. We can settle any disputes or issues then. Agreed?"

The dark figure pauses for a moment, "What you propose sounds like fun. We will have to do that. Of course, you are no match for me. Give yourself another several years. Then you might be of some competition. Until then . . ."

The dark figure disappears in a cloud of soot and ash.

'Verbally sparing with the Devil is never recommended!' Echoes within Marckolius' mind.

"You do understand I can see your shape most of the time. You were standing behind me instead of in front of me."

'I collect the souls you dispatch. I'm not really the guardian type. That is how it works.'

"I guess the rest is up to me?" Marckolius chuckles, "Next time show some back bone. There is work to be done."

'You have work to do? You've been on a vacation from life.'

"Then I guess our vacation is over. The real work is about to begin!"

CHAPTER 12

ALWAYS YOUR UNCLE!

THE TRANSPORT IS OLD AND dingy. Five caskets sit in the cargo hold with Marckolius, Viktorlo, and Brianto. Their thick black wool robes match the décor. The sounds of the engines reverberate through the cargo hold making it very hard to hear anything.

Marckolius reaches into his right pocket and pulls out six small blue crystals. "Here are three crystals for each of you." He yells so they can hear him. "They are one use only. Once used, they will dissolve into dust. They will work on any door or computer system in the palace. Just be careful with them."

"We don't get a copy of your key?" Viktorlo yells even though he is within inches of Marckolius.

"This is the best Kismet could do for us on such short notice."

"I wish I had brought ear plugs with me. I can barely hear myself think," Yells Brianto.

The engine noise dies down to a loud hum. "We have just come out of Interdimensional Space. We should be landing shortly." Marckolius leans back against the wall of the cargo hold. "Just stick to your assignments."

Viktorlo leans into Marckolius, "I am picking up the last items from my parents' vault in the palace."

"I know." Marckolius closes his eyes. "Everyone will think you came there to do that instead of the real mission."

"Do I get to blow the depot or what?" Brianto jokes. "I almost accidentally did it a few years ago. I figure I should get a second crack at it."

"No loss of life!" Stresses Marckolius. "Let me remind you, we will have one hour from when we disembark to get back to this ship. Otherwise we will be using the gate to get back to Gregoria."

"We know!" Brianto puts up the heavy dark wool hood of his robe. "You know this stuff itches like crazy."

"It's the latest fashion for undertakers." Viktorlo puts his hood up.

Marckolius puts his hood up as well. "We are here. Just try to act like undertakers. And, get those black skin tight gloves on."

The ship touches down with a heavy thud, shaking the caskets. "Good thing they were strapped down." Brianto starts to undo the straps.

They finish undoing the straps as the cargo door opens. Guards enter quickly. They inspect the cargo hold. Marckolius, Viktorlo, and Brianto stand by, motionless. The guards ignore them without hesitation.

The captain of the ship enters with a digital pad, "As you can see there are five caskets and three undertakers."

The lead guard signs the digital pad. "It shows here you are bringing back one casket?"

"That is right, dropping off five, and picking up one." The captain allows two more undertakers to pass. "They had to ride with me because of the number of caskets."

"Do your business and then go." The guards leave the ship.

"You heard the guard, move it. Each of you, get these deads off the ship." The captain stands off to the side to let them pass.

They move the caskets in a single file line toward the far side of the castle. With the morning sun showing brightly, they arrive at the high walls of the cemetery. Standing at the gate is a short lumpy man in dirty overalls and a skullcap.

"Five just as expected. Take them in." The caretaker opens the cemetery gate. "I got the update this morning that one dead was being removed. That is sort of unusual." No response comes from the undertakers. "You things don't talk much do you? Well, I see the number but who is going to pay the fee?"

Marckolius reaches out with his black rubber gloved hand releasing a small wool bag into the open hand of the caretaker. The caretaker opens the bag and counts the gold pieces.

"One thousand credits, more than double the fee. Be quick about it." The caretaker walks back into the building.

The undertakers move the five caskets into the building.

"Hey, one minute," The caretaker walks over to the undertakers, "The dead you are removing is in an unmarked grave with no grave identification or family to notify of the move. That is very unusual."

Marckolius steps forward saying in a growly voice, "Removing trash!"

The man steps back, "Then take the trash out of here. It's still in the ground. The shovels are over in the corner. We still do things the old-fashioned way. I will say you things don't talk much at all."

The undertakers grab the shovels and walk out of the room. They walk in single file to the plot with Marckolius leading the way. He stops at the plot and stomps his right foot. The others start digging. After a short while, they raise a pink and white casket. They clean off the dark dirt. Marckolius walks around it briefly. He bows to the others. Two of the undertakers take the casket back to the transport. Marckolius, Viktorlo, and Brianto walk back into the room. They walk past the now sleeping caretaker.

"You were right, that sleeping powder did put him out." Brianto takes off the robe.

"Remember, no killing. Try to be silent."

"You try to stay out of trouble yourself." Viktorlo pats Marckolius on the back.

Marckolius walks over to the far wall. He looks for a small hole near the lamp. He places his blue crystal into the hole. The crystal lights up momentary as the wall slides silently open.

"Funny how all those adventures we had growing up are paying off now." Marckolius removes the crystal.

They walk into the dimly lit passage. Viktorlo and Brianto go left. Marckolius walks straight ahead. The passage is very dirty as no one has been through it in many years. Cobwebs cover most of the corners. The passage wall silently closes behind them.

Marckolius finds the small elevator near the end of the hallway. He places his blue crystal into the socket. The small elevator comes to life. The door opens. He presses the top button making the elevator move quickly upward. It slowly stops. The door opens to his father's bedroom. He silently moves into the study. His father stands, gazing out the large ornate window overlooking the capital city.

"Hello father," Marckolius starts in a solemn tone. "How have you been?"

His father turns quickly with a look of surprise. "I, I, I, I, I," swallowing hard, "I am doing fine." A look of fear replaces the look of surprise upon his face.

"Fear father? What do you have to be so afraid of?" Marckolius takes several steps forward. "I'm not here to kill you if that is what you're thinking. If I wanted you dead you already would be."

"Then why have you come?" His father's shaky voice comes out weak.

"I came to talk to you, mostly to say goodbye."

"Goodbye?"

Marckolius takes a deep breath, "Yes, goodbye. I doubt I will ever see you again, at least face to face. But, I wanted to make you this promise." Marckolius walks forward to look his father in the eyes. "I will never move against the Proprietorship for as long as you are King. I promise you, never! This way my half-brothers and you will keep your positions within the Proprietorship."

"You didn't come just to tell me this. Why else are you here?"

"I came to take my mother home."

"Home, you mean Gregoria?" The sound of disgust comes from his father.

"Yes Gregoria, she was never given a proper burial. She wasn't even given a Queen's funeral. She was buried like some underpaid kitchen staff or guard. How could you do that to the woman you claimed to love?"

"I did what I could."

"Really, you did all you could? Don't lie to me. You covered up for my uncle." Marckolius' anger comes to the surface.

"I had to."

"Why? Do you know my uncle claimed it was a rich divorce? He said that during our fight when he blew up the table."

His father shakes his head no, "I would never rich divorce your mother. Yes, we grew apart while she had taken sanctuary on Gregoria after your birth. That year I took a lover without her permission. She ultimately became your step mother."

"Who had an accident when it was found she was having an affair with my uncle. Or should I call it an assassination?"

"Oh," his father takes several steps back. "You know about that."

"It's called a rich divorce! How convenient this happens for you, twice."

"Your uncle did it without me knowing. I knew you had told the truth. I knew your uncle was behind it but what could I do? He has always been the power behind the throne. I am more of an administrator. The Proprietorship holds all the real power." Hanging his head low, he sits in the well-padded chair next to his dark wooden desk.

"The last real King was your grandfather Merlinus. The scepter that encased the Master Key was destroyed when your grandfather's experiment caused him to disappear without a trace. The only survivor was his lab assistant, who disappeared shortly thereafter. I never had the Master Key."

"But you allowed me to be banished when I had done what I was instructed to do."

"I had no choice with that either. You have to believe me. Anyways, it was for your own good."

Marckolius ponders for a moment, "You do know that I will ultimately kill my uncle."

A gasp is heard from the front room, "Father!" A teen's voice echoes. In walks Nickolius, the older of Marckolius' two half-brothers, "Guards!" He begins yelling as he runs out of the room into the hallway.

"You must go now. Take care of yourself and your friends," his father opens his arms.

Marckolius steps back from his father, "I hope you understand, with everything that has happened I would be in my rights to kill you. I might have forgiven you, but I cannot ever forget." Marckolius reenters the elevator.

"I never even knew that was there," his father says as the elevator door closes.

The sirens sound throughout the palace. The echo is very slight in the passageway. Marckolius stands by the entrance to the cemetery caretaker's work area.

"You are late." Marckolius motions for Viktorlo and Brianto to hurry.

"We weren't the ones that were found out." Viktorlo is carrying a small grayish briefcase.

"We did get everything and more. Now open the way out." Brianto bangs against the wall.

Marckolius places his blue crystal into the slot. The wall silently swings open. The caretaker is still asleep. They grab the wool robes, put them back on, and walk out into the cemetery. They look up to see the transport flying off without them.

"Nice," Brianto yells, "we missed our way out of here."

"You know what this means, don't you?"

"Yes Viktorlo, it means we have to use the underground to get to the gate room on the other side of the palace."

"Those things down there don't like people." Brianto points out.

"We killed plenty when we went on our adventures. We will just have to kill any that get in our way." Marckolius shrugs his shoulders.

"We really have to go before they start looking for us." Viktorlo rushes back into the room. Marckolius and Brianto follow. Marckolius reopens the passageway door. They enter the passageway with the door closing behind them. They remove the brown wool robes, leaving them in a pile.

"We need to go down. It's this way." Marckolius leads them down the long passage, past the elevator, to a set of winding steps.

They move as silently as possible until they reach a large metal door. The controls next to the metal door look burnt out.

"Now what?" Brianto sits on the steps.

Marckolius pulls the controls off the wall. He reaches into the wall with his blue crystal. After several moments, the door clicks open only slightly. "Happy?"

They pull the door open. The smell of dampness hangs in the air. Sounds echo from different places below. A set of wet looking stone steps go down to their right.

"I had forgotten how bad this place smells." Viktorlo covers his nose with his hand.

Marckolius pulls out a small hand light as Brianto pulls the door closed. They slowly make their way down the steps to the damp floor.

"You remember the way?" Viktorlo asks Marckolius.

Marckolius smiles, "I think I know how to cut the power to palace. Let's get to the electric depot."

"Now you're talking. We can hit the power transformers midway through to the other side." Brianto smiles broadly.

They move as quickly as possible through the maze of tunnels and passageways. They only come across large furry rats.

"Where are the things that live down here?" Viktorlo asks aloud. "We should have run across something."

"These passages haven't been used in a long time." Brianto continues to look behind them as they move forward.

They come to a large open area with heavy fencings. Large metallic cylinders with large coils and cables protrude upward.

"We are at the midway point. Brianto, here is your depot!" Marckolius gestures.

"Not what I had originally wanted to take out. That time was an accident with that blasted ogre but this will do." Brianto pulls out his battle-ax. He swings down through the fencing. Orange and yellow sparks fly about. He does this twice more making a large opening. He walks up to the power console, pulls out a blue crystal, inserts it, and begins pressing a sequence of keys.

Viktorlo nudges Marckolius, "You know we haven't even run across any bones or anything. Maybe they are staying down in the really old vault areas?"

"I'm wondering about that myself. I was meaning to ask you, what's in the briefcase?"

"I don't know. It won't open."

"I'm done!" Brianto smashes the console with his axe. "These electrical transformers will overload in thirty minutes."

"Then we better move." They follow Marckolius out of the depot area into another set of long passageways.

They continue to move quickly until they reach a deep cavern. They look down to see the bones and carcasses of many dead animals. Loud growls and screeches echo from deep in the caverns far below.

"Mystery solved, I guess." Marckolius looks down with his light. "Those were killed with weapons fire." He points to the blast marks about the area. "Looks like a salvage operation."

They continue to move on until they reach an area near their exit. Two shadowy figures stand in black within the corners of the room where they blend into the shadows.

Marckolius stops Viktorlo and Brianto from entering, "There are two of them in there. Do you feel the demonic presence with them?"

"Why are the Duad Bantam guarding the way up to the gate room?" Viktorlo puts the gray briefcase down.

"We don't have long before the electric depot goes boom." Brianto reminds them.

"Let's get this over with." Marckolius leads the way into the room.

The two members of the Duad Bantam dodge the first several shots only to fall. Their bodies explode in a shower of blood leaving their black clothes in blood soaked piles on the stone floor.

"Not very experienced were they?" Marckolius comments.

"When did your father start to hire assassins to guard the palace?"

"I doubt he knows about it. I bet my uncle hired them."

"Everything is always your uncle." Brianto wipes his battle-ax off.

"Let's go! Our last visit back is over." Marckolius slips his blue crystal into the hole next to the door console. The wall slides open.

Back on Gregoria, the analysis of the captured data begins. An analyst in light brown robes briskly enters, "Sirs, pardon but you must come and see this."

All three follow the analyst to a large circular room with digital wall screens displaying star charts and ships. The holographic table in the center shows a path zigzagging through two galaxies with Gregoria close to the end.

Marckolius stares at the holographic image. "How long do we have before they get here?"

"We have maybe a year, most likely less," the analyst states.

"Viktorlo, we have six months to build that fleet we talked about."

Viktorlo shakes his head, "Six months to build a fleet to take on your uncle? You've got to be kidding me!"

"Assemble our allies and those we trust. We will present this information to them. My uncle is coming and it's up to us to stop him!"

"It looks like Remos is two stops before us. And the end is Elkri?" Viktorlo looks in closer. "He's stopping at the first kingdom in the Eugenitor's territory. They will start full-blown genocide in retaliation."

Brianto shakes his head, "Damn, it is always your uncle!"

CHAPTER 13

TRANSITION

"**E**NOUGH!" MARCKOLIUS POUNDS THE LARGE table before him with his fist. "Do you understand what is going to happen if we do nothing?" Representatives from multiple planets all stop. They stare at Marckolius. "We returned with this information a month ago. All you've done these past several days is argue and argue. If we do nothing then we doom those we are sworn to protect!"

A half man, half cat walks forward. His golden armor glistens under the lights of the large conference hall. His brownish fur stands on end. "We are the strongest military here. We should lead. We should be the ones to dictate the terms to everyone else. You should bow to us!"

The uproar begins again. "You are a Felini, the Prince? I see your sister standing with Viktorlo over there."

A look of anger flashes across his face. "We are leaving this mess. Contact us when you are ready to submit to our rule." He grabs his similarly dressed sister and leaves.

"I am King Marston of Remos." An older man with a grayish beard walks forward. His gold and silver armor clinks as he moves. "We have no intentions of letting anyone create a theocracy throughout these galaxies." Many in the room verbally agree with him.

Marckolius walks from the front of the room to face King Marston directly. "I have no intentions of setting up a theocracy anywhere."

"You answer to the Gregorian Larch, don't you?" Marckolius does not answer. "Well then, I say until you, your friends, and the warriors called Warrior Priests no longer answer to the Gregorian Larch, we have nothing to discuss."

He turns his back and starts to walk out of the room. Many others start to follow him.

"I would like to make something known before you physically walk out." Marckolius yells loud enough to catch everyone's attention. They turn, "If you walk out of here right now I tell you as war comes we will not defend any of you. We will only defend those that stand with us. I swear unto God we will stand!"

King Marston walks back to Marckolius, "You talk, but you cannot escape the reality of this situation. The forces you are building answer to the church."

"I do see your point. However, our forces stand to defend, not conquer. If any of you doubt what my uncle will do to you let me explain it. He will pillage your planets." Marckolius strides through the room, facing each delegate. "He will rape your planets! When he's finished, if your people have no further value to the Proprietorship, he will destroy your planets! If you think you can pay him off, if you think you can bribe him, if you think you can satisfy him, you are all wrong!" Marckolius continues making his way through the delegates. "I know the Proprietorship. I know what they want. I know what they will do to each planet. They don't care about your people. They don't care about how much damage they cause. They least care if they kill all of you. The Proprietorship cares about; credits, money, wealth, gold, precious metals, and technology. Does any of that have to do with your survival?"

A long silence lies upon the room like a heavy fog. Marckolius walks back to the front. No one moves or makes a single noise.

"It is not my intention to fear monger or scare you into joining us. I am telling you the truth. I am telling you the reality of the situation. If we stand together, we will stop him. If we remain divided then that evil dog will pick each of you off one by one, making his forces stronger." Marckolius clenches his fist in front of himself.

Marckolius points to the door, "You doubt what I say, leave! Find out for yourselves what happens when you try to deal with the Proprietorship. The Felini have left. They believe themselves strong. They will find out the hard way. The rest of you have a choice to make.

Make it quickly because time is one commodity we cannot afford to waste."

"We will let you know." King Marston states. Many others voice the same as they leave the room.

"You did the best you could." Viktorlo walks up. "You've started building the fleet with your own money, however much it might be. But we can't go it alone."

"I don't think we will be alone. We do have some allies. As for now our work is still quite daunting."

The Lord General stops Marckolius, "I would like to speak with you for a moment."

"Sure, anything for you."

"Walk with me Marckolius. I have a meeting with the Church Council and would like you to accompany me." They leave the room together, walking slowly down the vacant corridor. Guards follow. "I saw what you were doing in there. A great first attempt but they are right. In order to do this you cannot answer to your grandfather. Those forces you are building cannot answer to the church. And, you must have some type of undisputed authority."

"I will think up some type of political solution."

"Let me ask you a question, do you know the word that cannot be spoken?" The Lord General's frail voice becomes apparent.

"There are several words that cannot be spoken."

"I am talking about the word that is a place we cannot go. A word that is in the back of every human's mind but they cannot touch it. They cannot speak it."

Marckolius ponders as he walks, "I know the word."

"You do?" They stop. "Does it still exist?"

"It is enveloped in flame, souls in perpetual anguish."

"Did you see him?" He whispers into Marckolius' ear.

"We had a cordial conversation out on the training grounds after you had left that first day. He warned me never to access his realm again."

"Ahhh, then he must not be able to kill you." The Lord General continues to whisper.

"We will meet one day, in the place between Heaven and Hell to fight."

They start walking again. "You find yourself between a rock and hard place right now. Trust me, I have your solution." They walk until they reach a golden elevator. "Do you know why the Lord General answers to the Gregorian Larch?"

"If memory serves, it is because the Gregorian government fell during the Anarchy Wars many centuries past. The church took over the military and forced a strict moral code over them. They turned them into Warrior Priests, in name only."

"Are you a priest or a warrior?" The elevator doors open. Both enter.

"Neither."

"Does Gregoria have a government?"

"Gregoria has a democratically elected government but they are overridden by the Church Council all the time. The Church Council has the final say over everything."

"How do you feel about that?"

"If I may speak freely, sir?" The Lord General nods, "This has turned into a thug-ocracy. All theocracies eventually turn into one. It's a poor form of socialism that never works. That's why we have fuel shortages, high unemployment, high taxes, and bad relations with everyone. Gregoria is weak, predictable, and has a superiority complex that most loath. The only way to manage resources is to develop them. That includes people. We must teach them to think and do for themselves and to become what God has intended for them to be. You cannot expect people to be creative and prosper when the government dictates almost every facet of their lives."

The elevator stops with the doors opening to the underground Church Council Room. "Perfect young man, you keep that attitude for as long as you live."

The Lord General walks forward until he is in the center of the half circle table. He looks at the Gregorian Larch and bows. Marckolius stands off to the side in the back of the room.

"My old friends," The Lord General begins. "I have lived three life time's now. I am two hundred and eighty-five years old. I do not intend to continue in this position any longer. Thus, I am retiring effective immediately." Most of the Church Council remains silent. "As is my right, I have picked my successor, Marckolius."

"NO!" Many of the Church Council stands in protest.

The Gregorian Larch stands, putting forth his hands. The council members quietly sit, "My old friend, why my grandson?"

"Because he, of everyone I know, has the leadership, knowledge, and skill for this position. He has revamped our training methods. He has organized the building of the new fleet, despite resistance from this council. He moves forward, always moving forward. He has matured much since I first met him many years ago. Most of all, he is unencumbered by the current political and social status quo. What we need is new leadership with vision and that is Marckolius."

"I see. It is your right under our law for you to pick your successor. However, he must be able to state the word to us without speaking it. Given this requirement, Marckolius step forward and give us the word." The Gregorian Larch sits down.

Marckolius walks forward, still with a look of surprise. He slightly bows to his grandfather. He looks at the council members. Many of them show disgust and disdain. Some show fear.

"I am just as surprised as all of you. I did not accompany him down here with the knowledge that I would be picked to become the Lord General."

"That is all fine and dandy!" One of the council members stand, "Do you or don't you know the word?"

Marckolius looks at everyone in the room, "I would advise you to sit back down."

"He doesn't know the word," Taunts another.

A burst of psychic energy pulses from Marckolius. The word is spoken loudly in each of their minds, which also causes the one council member standing to fall to the floor.

"I did warn you." Marckolius starts. "But why should the word not be spoken a loud? Is it evil? Is it an affront to God? No! Why hide our origin? Are you still embarrassed? It has been five thousand years since this church played a role in the place of origin for seven civilizations of man being sent straight into the first level of Hell!"

"My grandson, do not lecture the members of this council. You have proven you know the word and your psychic ability."

"Grandfather, and members of this council," Marckolius sternly looks throughout the room. "I will not answer to this council."

"What? How dare you!?!" Council members stand and yell.

'Remember the promise made . . .'

"Sit down!" Marckolius forces them to sit with his words echoing through their minds. "You remember your place. This council is responsible for leading the church not all of the Gregoria and what is left of her colonies. It's time you focused on rejuvenating the church. I will focus on a restoration of the full Gregorian government. I have no intentions of ruling if that is what you fear. I intend on keeping a promise made by this church hundreds of years ago to reconstitute the government once order was restored after the Anarchy Wars. You focus on saving souls by winning their hearts and minds."

The Gregorian Larch stands and looks at the now former Lord General visibly upset, "You knew he would do this."

"My old friend, it is time for the promise to be kept. He is the one to do this for us. He is strong while we are weak."

"My suggestion to you is to stick to matters of morality and faith. Leave politics to the politicians. When you mix the two you damage what little credibility you have left."

"We can stop you!" Comes from one council member.

Another council member yells, "We know how to kill your kind!"

"Yes, I am a destroyer. Yes, I have killed many but never in cold blood. Don't any of worry, I do not intend to start now. Of course, if any of you are stupid enough to engage in assassination attempts," Marckolius looks each of them in eyes, "I will execute you for treason! Understood?" After a short pause, "Good, if you all will excuse me, I believe we are now in a state of transition."

Marckolius bows slightly to his grandfather, turns, and enters the golden elevator with the now former Lord General.

CHAPTER 14

RECIPROCATION

WORD MOVES FAST THROUGH THE warrior ranks and the church. The coming weeks give way to a transitional government. Marckolius sits in his living room with a single light emanating from the pad he is reading. His eyes become droopy.

'*Stay awake.*' Marckolius hears in his head.

"Why? Maybe if I sleep on this I will solve the power core issues. We just cannot generate enough power for those ships. They are too big."

'*DANGER!*'

Marckolius closes his eyes while reaching out psychically around his condominium. His eyes reopen lighting up the area with a red hue.

"I feel the demonic presence, one above on the roof and the other in the vent above my bedroom."

The anger he feels wakes him fully. He grabs his sword in time to see the assassin from the roof swinging down into the very large picture window. The assassin smashes through the window impaling himself upon Marckolius' sword. The assassin lets out a loud yelp as the glass shards fall around them. A burst of dark energy releases and dissipates. The smell of rotting flesh hits Marckolius. He sees the assassin gasp out a last breadth from a decayed face.

"Oh no!" Marckolius notices some type of bomb vest on the assassin. He spins himself around releasing the dead assassin out the window. He jumps behind the couch as the bomb blows, shattering all of the windows on that side of the building. Shrapnel cuts through the couch, darting past him and landing on the thick carpet.

"That was a very old assassin." Marckolius shakes off some remains of the couch.

'The other one.'

The putrid smell of decaying flesh nauseates Marckolius. He gets up in time to see the other assassin running towards him. He parries the blow, spinning the assassin into the wall. The assassin's shadow screeches with the hit from Marckolius' sword.

"You guys smell really bad."

The assassin comes at him again. Marckolius knocks the weapon from his hand, spins, and slices into his left arm. Little blood comes from the wound. The assassin takes several steps back, his eyes a milky white.

"We send greetings from your uncle!" The assassin growls as he rips his black shirt off to show a bomb vest.

Marckolius lunges with his sword, impaling him through his heart. With a burst of dark energy dissipating, he can see the rotting flesh of the dead assassin. The lights on the bomb vest start blinking faster and faster. Marckolius tosses the body into the bedroom and runs.

'Jump!'

Marckolius jumps out of the living room window. The shockwave of the detonation pushes him farther and farther out. The smoke and debris swallows him.

'Roll to your back.'

Marckolius rolls in time to feel the shock of his back hitting a large solid window. The shards cut through his cloths into his flesh. The shock spreads through his body leaving him in a state of pain he has never felt before. He hits the hard floor rolling repeatedly until he stops against the far wall. He lays bleeding, unable to move, unable to think, unable to do anything at all.

Darkness surrounds him. Slowly he sees a light blue grid. The sound of soft crying catches his attention. He moves forward, the echo of each step piercing his mind. He sees a women sitting on the grid looking down over Gregoria. He stops short kneeling down a couple meters away from her. Her dull red hair flows down her back. Her pail glittery skin makes her look frail. Her white nightgown floats around her. Tears roll down her pail cheeks. Her aura is a very light pink.

"Are you okay? Is something wrong?" He asks.

She turns slightly to Marckolius. "Why would you care?" She inquires.

"I ask because you look ill. You look frail and weak."

"Well, if you must know, I am. My father is bringing me here." She points at the planet.

"You are looking at Gregoria. They have the best medical technology in this known universe." He moves slightly closer to her. "You are a Eugenitor? Don't Eugenitors euthanize the sick and infirm when they cannot cure them?"

"Yes, my father has spent much of our family wealth bringing me here in one last attempt to cure me."

"What is your name?"

"I don't really know any more. I've been in stasis for so long it is hard for me to know." Her tears roll down her face, dropping on her lap.

"If I am to help you I must know your name."

"Why would you help me? You don't even know me."

"It's the right thing to do. If I can help I want to help."

"You don't look so good yourself, you know." She jokes.

"I know. I just survived another attempt on my life. I think I am suffering from a concussion. But, I ended up here for a reason."

She smiles slightly, "My name is Zorina."

"That is a very unique name. You wouldn't be Princess Zorina of Elkri, would you?"

"You know who I am but I do not know who you are."

"I am Marckolius."

"You have a unique name too, oh, the banished one." She wipes the last of her tears. "I must be going. We are about to arrive."

"You can tell?"

"I can listen, I just can't respond. I have heard much. But now I must go."

She slowly dissolves away before him.

"Alright Ophion, you can come out now," Marckolius says.

Ophion seems to walk out from behind a close by planet. He helps Marckolius to his feet.

"You seem to be injured quite badly. First time you felt your true mortality?"

"While I'm here I might as well check up on my uncle." With a wave of his hand the perspective changes, before him a large fleet of ships bombarding a small planet causing great destruction of the surface. "My uncle looks busy." A smaller silver ship jets out from behind the Cerci, his uncle's command ship. "I have never seen a ship like that before." He turns to Ophion.

Ophion stands beside him with wide eyes. Anger shows upon his face. "I must go. You should return and make sure you get the medical attention you need. Be sure to take care of that girl."

"Who does that ship belong to?"

"This changes everything! I will be in contact with you soon."

Ophion quickly dissolves away.

Marckolius opens his eyes. People are running beside him as they are pushing him through very bright hallways.

A women covered in a red tight gown leans over him, "You are going to be alright Lord General."

He tries to speak but only gurgling sounds come out. His body aches with great pain.

Marckolius opens his eyes again to the feeling of harsh pinching and pulling from his backside.

"Hey, that hurts!" He barks out.

"Oh good, he's awake." Brianto hops over to him. "You scared us."

Clink . . .

"Owwwwww!!!! Hey, try using some pain killer back there!"

"I thought this would wake you up." The doctor behind him laughs.

"Nice doc, now how about some anesthetic?"

"You can't take the pain?"

"Owwwwwwwww!!!"

Clink . . .

"Suck it up, I'm almost done."

Marckolius cringes. Clink . . .

"Everyone here is absolutely shocked you survived that blast. The plasma bomb took the top quarter off of the building." Brianto tries to show how much of the building was blown off using his hands.

Clink . . .

"Ready for the big one?" The doctor chuckles.

"Alright."

"On three, one . . ."

"Owwwwwwwwwwwwwwwwww!!!!!"

Clank . . .

"I thought you said on three."

"I lied," the doctor chuckles. "I just need to bandage up the slits in your ass and I will be done."

"Gee, thanks," Marcolius notices Brianto laughing, "Just wait until we got to pull something out of your ass."

"I'm sorry but you have no idea how funny this whole thing is. I just wish Viktorlo was here."

"Where is he anyways?"

"He had something to do with the fleet."

The doctor finishes up, taking the red skintight rubber gloves off his hands. "I have to ask you to please rest for the next couple days, even though I know you won't. You have a grade 3 concussion. That hard head of yours helped you survive. You really do need to stay off your feet, at least for the rest of the day. No heavy exertion, fighting, killing assassins, you know, the usual, for the rest of the week."

"Thanks doc, you're as funny as in the past." They shake hands.

"Really though, try to rest. Take care Marcolius." The doctor exits the room through the thick steel doors.

After a short pause, "Now then, where is Viktorlo?"

"He's following up on an intelligence report showing that your uncle has purged the Syndicate of all those loyal to you. Anna, Darling, and Telibina are missing." Brianto words trail off.

"I know how much you care about Telibina. This is disturbing but it was expected."

Brianto sits down, hanging his head low. "I didn't think I would be this worried about her but I am. I think I love her."

"Everyone can tell. They will turn up. Probably where you least expect it." After a long pause, "I need you to check on the arrival of King Artamus from Elkri. He is bringing his daughter Zorina here for treatment."

The confusion on Brianto's face gives way to an understanding look, "You've been at it again. Next time you go to the Celestial Plenum, please try looking for Telibina. I will check on King Artamus' arrival with his daughter."

"And, prep a private briefing room some place close to them. I will limp in and out if I have to. This is very important. And try to get me something for this headache."

"Yeah, I'll also check with Viktorlo for an update. Later . . ." Brianto exits through the steel doors.

Marckolius reawakens to Brianto shaking him. "Come on, sleep time is over." He hands him two pills.

"What, I dosed off again?" Marckolius swallows the pills.

"Yes you did. The guards have been checking in on you. That concussion must be affecting your senses."

"They're here in the medical center. Has King Artamus requested a meeting yet?"

"Yep, it's time to go. I brought you some clothes. All we had is your spare military uniform from the High Command facility. It will have to do."

"Thanks. I'll be out in a few," Marckolius dresses quickly. He limps from the room, the guards following closely. Brianto leads him to the far side of the medical center.

"This is what you asked for, a private briefing room close by to King Artamus and Princess Zorina."

The pale small room has only a few chairs and a small round table. The guards bring a plush chair.

"The soft chair should be easy on your rump." Brianto smirks holding back a giggle.

Marckolius gives him a quick dirty look. "This will do. Bring King Artamus when he's ready."

King Artamus enters the room with a doctor in tow. His simple dark red and brown clothes match his beard of red hair and thinning hairline. His dark complexion shows aging. He sits across from Marckolius. The doctor sits next to him.

"I heard about the attempt on your life. You barely escaped from what I was told." King Artamus begins, "I wanted to ask you for your help with a very private matter."

"Your daughter is ill. I know you brought her here at great expense, violating many of the rules laid down by your Eugenitor overlords." Marckolius sits up in his chair to look at King Artamus eye to eye. "How may I help with this?"

"If I may?" The doctor chimes in. With a nod from King Artamus he begins, "Princess Zorina is suffering from a very rare blood illness. She is deteriorating very rapidly. The only cure we found is your blood. You see, you were exposed to this blood illness when you were very young. You developed antibodies that should cure her."

Marckolius ponders for a moment. "I was exposed when I was very young. That could only mean vampirism. It's not an illness, it's a blood disease. It genetically changes you into a vampire. There are only a couple of cures for it. But, Eugenitors are immune to it."

"Not in this case," King Artamus sits back in his chair. "Her mother became infected before she was born. She changed while still pregnant. She died after birth."

"So you need my blood?" He looks at the doctor, "You brought what you need?"

"I've heard you are not so easy to pull blood from. Your wounds are probably healed by now."

"Give me the syringe," Marckolius commands. He takes it and jabs it into the vein in his left arm. It fills quickly. With a press of the top, a sizzle noise occurs. He takes it away to show a small mark on his arm. The mark from the syringe disappears before their eyes. "Is this enough?"

"Yes it is. I will go and start the process immediately." The doctor exits the room.

"I want to thank you for this," King Artamus smiles. "Anything I can do to repay this I will."

'Bio-Generator' Marckolius hears in his mind. It jogs his memory of an old story he once heard.

"I remember something about a bio-core or bio-generator experiment that the Eugenitors tried many decades ago." The smile on King Artamus' face disappears. "We don't want the prototype locked up in your vaults. We only want the schematics."

"Why!?!" King Artamus angrily asks. "That horrible device was fed tens of thousands ordered to be euthanized. It is a device thought up by the devil and given to our overlords."

"You don't understand. We are not going to recreate the device. We are only interested in the enhancements or modifications. We need to modify our energy cores. We can't generate enough power right now to have a full on battle with my uncle."

"You are asking for something that is sealed away, never to be thought of again!" King Artamus stands, "I cannot give you what you want. I am sorry." He turns to leave.

"My uncle's last stop on his tour of rape and pillaging is Elkri. You cannot stop him but we can. We just need those schematics." After a short pause, "I was hoping you would reciprocate my saving of your daughter's life with helping us save four other fully populated worlds, besides Gregoria and Elkri."

King Artamus turns back to Marckolius, "I am aware of your uncle's tour of destruction. I will get you the schematics. Just remember, you will have to deal with the consequences of using them."

"That's all I am asking for. Thank you."

King Artamus nods, turns and exits the room.

CHAPTER 15

WE WILL REALLY SURPRISE THEM

MANY WEEKS PASS. MARCKOLIUS ENTERS the power generation testing facility. The huge round room is a larger replica of the sealed housing that protects the power cores on the war ships they are building. Monitoring equipment encircle the round core in the center of a floor to ceiling conduit.

"I am glad that you made it," Kismet greets Marckolius.

"You said there was progress with our power issues."

They walk down to the core, "We've made modifications to the current cores so they will more than quadruple the power output. One core can now take the place of several. We won't need all the cores after all."

"Yes we will. You see, being able to fire all of the weapons, maneuver, and have unlimited power for the shields will make us near impossible to defeat. That's the idea behind this. I do have to ask, what are we using for fuel?"

"Heavy solar gravitons embedded in the deep solar plasma from the chromospheres. We create a highly pressurized magnetic bottle with a standard rotation state. The center filament extracts the energy while we feed in hydrogen. We can refill the cores no matter the . . ." Kismet stops talking when he notices Marckolius staring into the chamber. "What are you looking at?"

"I noticed something. The initial chain reaction to start the fission will cause a gravitational field burst that would blow the magnetic bottle."

"That's why we created the self-perpetuating feedback loop. As long as we keep extracting the excess energy from the core there isn't an issue."

"I see, so how do you compensate for the helium exhaust?"

"It gets burned off through the . . ."

"It's absorbed through the magnetic bottle and fed into the primary weapons cannon along with the plasma. When helium is not needed, it is collected into pressurized tanks for later use. No exhaust from the ships means you can't trace them through ID Space or normal space. Once all the tanks are full we would have to stop and expel the gas, most likely into a nearby sun to burn off all traces."

"If you knew the answers then why do you ask questions?" Kismet sounds upset.

"Sorry but the design modifications you made are a combination of the cores from the Proprietorship and that evil bio-core. The only way to make it work is a self-perpetuating feedback loop. I guess it would make for a handy self-destruct mechanism too. When we enter ID Space you better double the strength of the magnetic bottle. Solar plasma is directly affected by Interdimensional gravity waves."

"But we made it all work!"

"You did. I couldn't make it work but you did. I just read the brief and some additional information on solar mechanics. It's a strategy I used in the past, causing solar waves and flares in battle. The enemy is always caught off guard."

"I underestimated you. You are far more devious that I thought."

"Thank you for the back handed compliment. When will these new cores be put into the ships?"

"That is being done right now. Furthermore, the others have agreed to join us. We will have enough Cerebria here in the next day to become each of the ships. They are learning the dialects and speech patterns so they will better mesh with crews."

"You convinced them?"

"They were convinced by the chance to work with you. I only had to ask for volunteers. I will be the command ship."

"I'm honored but I thought you were the ambassador to Gregoria?"

"We have been monitoring events across the galaxy. I want you to consider what will happen once you defeat your uncle. Think about what comes next. You will come to the next logical conclusion just as our entire race has. We want in on what will be a new future."

"Once again I think you're a few steps ahead of where I am right now."

"And you haven't thought about filling the power vacuum after this is done?"

The alarms start to go off. Marckolius accesses the nearby terminal. "An unidentified stealth fighter has entered Gregoria and is demanding the right to land at the hanger bay to the High Command. I guess I am saved by the alarm bell. Sorry but I have to get up there."

"You and I will need to complete this conversation," Kismet calls after Marckolius.

Marckolius gets to the hanger bay to find Brianto arguing with his aunt.

"Fill me in, what is going on?" Marckolius interrupts them.

"He granted the fighter permission to land," Sister Marianus exclaims as she pokes Brianto in the chest. "And he is preventing us from taking the pilot into custody."

Marckolius looks at Brianto, "Well?"

"It's Telibina. The pilot is Telibina. I recognized her intelligence code."

"Then this is a matter for the High Command, not the Demon Hunters." Marckolius turns to the guards, "Bring her here at once. And make sure she is uninjured."

"Delay that!" Sister Marianus storms in front of Marckolius. "She is a vampire. That makes it the domain of the Demon Hunters. By our agreement she is to be interrogated by us."

"She is an intelligence asset."

"No, she is Brianto's play thing," She counters, gritting her teeth.

Marckolius puts out his hand, stopping Brianto from moving toward his aunt. "If you do not relinquish I will relinquish for you. She is under our protection. You got that!"

"You say intelligence? Let's see this intelligence first before I agree to anything, nephew."

Marckolius pulls close to his aunt. He softly speaks, "Anna and the rest have been missing for weeks now. They were our intelligence sources within the Syndicate. They were feeding us detailed information on my uncle's progress, ship manifests, prisoners, everything you could think of. If Telibina is here that means she has detailed intelligence that could not wait. Understand?"

"I still want to see it. He isn't getting his play thing without proof."

Marckolius turns to the guards, "Bring Telibina to the private conference room on level 10. We will speak to her there." Sister Marianus nods in agreement.

Upon entering the conference room Telibina runs up and hugs Brianto. Her vampire image blows away from her like grains of sand in the wind. Her long blond hair trails behind her. Her soft facial features show excitement. They passionately kiss.

"Get a room! We are here to see the intelligence information." Sister Marianus barks.

"You're Okay?" Brianto looks at her.

"I made it out alive. I can't say the same for my Mistress or Darling." Telibina places her head into Brianto's chest.

"Alright, please sit. Seal the room," Marckolius orders. Marckolius puts his right hand out toward Telibina, palm up. She timidly places a small orange crystal in his hand. "Thank you." He places the crystal into the reader.

Anna appears on the video screen. Fear is plainly visible upon her face, despite the fangs and darkish color skin. Her red hair looks frizzy and unwashed. "Hello Marckolius. If you are getting this, it means I didn't make it out of here. Your uncle is coming to purge the Syndicate. We have no real way of stopping it. I know it was only a matter of time. We have been preparing for this. Listen carefully, on this crystal are detailed intelligence showing your uncle's modified attack plans as filed with the Proprietorship. He is skipping Calabra. This means he will be at Remos in four weeks. The Proprietorship ordered the shifting in his plans. Calabra paid almost a trillion credits to be taken off the list. They also promised to work with the Proprietorship to gather intelligence."

Marckolius pauses the screen, "Notify Viktorlo to round up the Calabra." Brianto nods and exits the room.

"How do you know what she says is accurate?" Sister Marianus sits with her hand on a stake, never taking an eye off Telibina.

"I trust her."

"Why, because you two . . ."

119

"Shut it!" Telibina yells. "You are a grouchy old hag with no love in your heart. You know nothing of my Mistress."

"Oh sure, and next you'll tell me you don't drink blood and kill small animals. You are the spawn of the devil, the whole lot!" Sister Marianus stops all movement.

Marckolius has reached his limit, "Sorry about doing that. You were not going to stop this incessant obsession unless I explain a little reality to you." Marckolius pushes his aunt back down into her chair. "Now, Telibina is a real vegetarian. Most of them are. Vampires are not the spawn of the devil, they are genetically altered by a blood disease called vampirism. You know these things but yet you still cling to the old superstitions. I will let you go if you promise to be civil. Promise?"

His aunt nods yes. He releases her. She looks angrily at him, "Don't do that again!"

"Then please quietly sit and listen to the rest of the message."

Telibina sits back in her chair with a wide smile on her face. His aunt sits angrily back with her arms crossed, still holding the stake in her hand.

Marckolius hits play, "There is also another race helping him with modifications. They are known as the Kaosians but I cannot guarantee the information. I am most sorry I will not be of any further help to you. I know you will succeed. I must go. Take care of yourself and your friends." The screen goes dark.

"Now I know what they're called," Marckolius comments aloud.

"Who, the Kaosians?" Sister Marianus asks.

"Do you know about them? I know what is rumbling around my head but it seems confusing."

"No! But I bet Ophion might."

"Who is Ophion and who are the Kaosians?" Telibina looks at both with confusion.

"I'll set someone to start researching it. But, on to your jurisdiction?"

"Fine, keep her; she's not worth anything to us. You make sure she doesn't leave Brianto's six meter radius." Sister Marianus stands.

"I don't believe that will be an issue. Will it Telibina?" Telibina shakes her head no with a big happy smile.

"Good, I do hope you give my best to grandfather. I haven't had much time to see him lately."

"Of course nephew, take care." She hugs him. She shoots Telibina an angry look as she leaves the room.

Brianto enters as Sister Marianus leaves. Telibina stands and hugs him.

"She cannot leave your six meter radius or she might be taken into custody or worse. Understand?"

"Yeah," Brianto answers. "Viktorlo needs you in the private conference room up a level. This is an emergency."

"It doesn't look like we are going to be able to save Remos. There isn't enough time to finish the ships or the battle prep. This information is a good two weeks old."

"Before you go," Telibina stops Marckolius at the door. "What about all the vampires that have no place to go? It's not just me that needs a place to stay. The others need a place as well."

"Can they be trusted not to indiscriminately kill? Would they follow our orders?"

"I believe so. I can create enough of the vege-blood to feed them. They are seasoned fighters and from what I can tell you need seasoned fighters."

"Brianto take care of this. Use the shipyards. They won't bother the Beztra."

'The emergency . . .'

"Later then," Marckolius dashes out the door, grabbing the small orange crystal.

He rushes into the conference room, leaving two security guards outside. The holographic table shows the current track of his uncle's fleet.

"Here's the data crystal from Telibina." He tosses the crystal to Viktorlo. "The message from Anna mentions that the next stop is Remos. I don't think we will be ready in time to stop them there." Viktorlo points to the gentleman in the far corner of the room. Marckolius recognizes him, "Ophion?" Marckolius quickly moves around the table to shake his hand.

Ophion remains in the chair, "It is a pleasure to see you in person."

"They took you out of hibernation?"

"Sit, the situation is serious." Ophion presses a serious of buttons on the table causing the display to focus on Remos.

"Remos? They are next on my uncle's tour of destruction."

"You need to make your stand at Remos!" Ophion looks very serious at Marckolius. "We are willing to assist."

"How would you assist?" Viktorlo asks. "The battle prep and the finishing up of the fleet will take two weeks. We haven't even put the fleet through its paces yet. You would have to bend time or something."

"And, the information on this crystal is at least two weeks old. We cannot rush this or cut corners. We also have to wait for the purged vampires from the Syndicate. I am going to use them as our boarding party on the Cerci."

"You have two weeks to complete your prep work before we leave," Ophion reiterates.

"You need to explain why." Marckolius returns the serious look.

"Did you know that there were survivors from Earth? And, where they escaped too?" Viktorlo and Marckolius look at each other briefly. Marckolius sits back in his chair, closing his eyes. "I see you guessed it, Remos."

"What is so important about a group of refugees from Earth? This plan is not strategically sound." Viktorlo looks upset.

"They are the survivors. Their civilization isn't 5,000 years old like it should be. When they went through the wormhole outside of Sol they were catapulted to just a few hundred years ago. They are as close to real unaltered humans as we can get. The information about what that means is in your head."

"Okay, we are supposed to figure out how to defend Remos when we cannot get there in time no matter how fast we complete anything. I am not cutting corners for their sake. You've got to understand, their King refused any assistance or we could have been ready by now."

"That's why I brought something. It is currently being installed into your command ship."

"What? What did you bring?"

"The device being installed into your ship will bend time to the point that that you will exit Interdimensional Space a microsecond later than when you entered. It is as close to simultaneous as you can get without causing a cataclysm." Viktorlo and Marckolius look at each other again. "Now then, you finish your prep work. I will converse with your engineers on how to use the device."

"Kismet is the command ship, once you install it he will know most everything about it." Marckolius states in a monotone voice.

Ophion's eyes widen, "You mean the Cerebria will become your ships? Do you know what you just did? You have given them the ability to exterminate all life in the Multiverse. You have no sense!"

"Excuse me but they're not going to do any such thing. Whatever distrusts and hatreds exist between the Cerebria and Galatics have no place here. There are cut offs and safeguards already in place. I trust Kismet. The Cerebria want to be part of this. They want to be part of the future."

"I hope to God you are right because if you aren't, then not even our technology will be able to stop them. Eons of conflict and now you decide to give it all away, no matter how old or wise they are at times."

"There is no AI ever created that could control those ships. Without the Cerebria we couldn't even get close to defeating my uncle. At some point, you have to trust in someone other than yourself and God. Until they show a reason not to trust them, they will be treated as an ally and friend."

Viktorlo taps the table showing an image of the internal structure, infrastructure, and systems of the ships they are building. "On to the ship design, the power cores will now put out more than four times their original output." The power core clusters light up in the holographic design of the ship. "The cannon is an updated version of the orbiting planetary cannons around Gregoria." The large size cannon with a large plasma collection base and filament light up. "The propulsion uses a phasing effect to enter Interdimensional Space." The back and lower parts of the ship light up showing a multitude of micro coils lining each layer of the hull. "The shields use a trilateral overlapping to take most blasts without loss of power." Lateral lines of shield emitters every twenty-four meters light up in the holographic display. "The cannon and power cores each have independent shielding giving us added protection from radiation given the bridge sits right behind the cannon." The two-story bridge light up directly behind the large cannons. "Not to mention the amount of cannon and missile batteries that line the hall."

Ophion stares at the rotating holographic view, "This design is near flawless. You have more power and protection than any previous warship I've ever seen."

"The designs and modifications are a merging of the best from each of our allies and friends." Marckolius smiles broadly with pride.

Ophion looks up at Marckolius, "I guess we will really surprise them."

CHAPTER 16

AT LONG LAST,
IT IS DONE!

THE COMMAND SHIP MOVES MAJESTICALLY from the shipyard, long, silver, and sleek with the largest mobile cannon ever built. A large thick flat wedge protrudes past the cannon on the front. Missile batteries and gun turrets cover much of the hull. The underside weapons surround the closing mini-ship bay. The ship is followed by thirty-nine slightly smaller but identical ships with primary cannons half the size of the command ship's cannon. The initials K.S. are clearly viewable on both side of the command ship.

Marckolius stands on the command deck looking across at the two-story concave front view screen. The sides of the bridge have similar viewing with flooring going half way to the center. The main section of the bridge is open for easy viewing from the chair in the very back of the bridge. Marckolius straightens his white uniform. The chair lights up when he sits down. Controls light up on both arms rests. The crystal sides of the chair glow with a pulsating blue that matches Marckolius' own eye color. Well-lit stairs go down to the lower deck of the bridge. Elevator doors are on both sides in the back corners.

Viktorlo walks up to Marckolius from the lower deck, "Your uncle's fleet just exited ID Space above Remos. We have plotted a course that will place us behind them."

Ophion exits from the right elevator with Brianto and Telibina. Ophion strokes his white beard, "Everything is ready. I still don't trust Kismet."

"He is listening. You do know that, right?" Marckolius jokes.

"You have nothing to fear from us Ophion." Kismet speaks through the above speaker, "We know our duty. We've been waiting eons for this."

The helmsman on the main deck stands and turns, "Sir, the Proprietor Fleet has just been engaged by the Remosians."

"That's our cue." Marckolius stands, "Slave the ships."

A holographic image of the fleet appears in the very center of the bridge. Light orange lines appear one after the other connecting the ships to K.S.

"Course is set," one of the helmsmen announces.

"Punch it!" Marckolius commands.

The countdown throughout the ship echoes, "Five, four, ready, steady, jumping into ID Space . . ."

A light vortex forms before K.S. instead of the usual dark and violent vortexes everyone is used to. The ships move forward into the vortex. The vortex expands, swallowing the entire fleet before collapsing into micro glittery space dust that swirls away into nothing. The representation on the screens of the bridge show a light white grid, eddies, vortexes, and other anomalies.

Ophion squints at the screens, "What is this being depicted?"

K.S. answers, "The eddies are suns, vortexes are black holes, and the other odd forms are other gravitational anomalies. This is how we see Interdimensional Space."

"It is far more comprehensive than anything we've ever seen before," Viktorlo states. "We can now see any object or ship. This gives us a distinct advantage."

"How long till we arrive at Remos in our time, not standard time?" Marckolius asks.

"Four hours, Sir," One of the helmsmen answers.

"Get the boarding parties ready. Bring up the two Commanders. It's time to clue them in on our boarding plan," Marckolius orders.

"One thing I noticed," Brianto interjects. "There was no jolt or odd feeling when we entered ID Space."

Ophion strokes his beard, "It must be the combination of the new micro propulsion coils and the black box."

"I don't care, it was different and unexpected." Brianto smiles, "less potential damage to our ships."

"I'll see the two Commanders while I change into my fighting gear." Marckolius changes his mind as he stands up. "K.S., you continue to monitor the situation on Remos. It would be nice to know every move they attempt."

"Of course, I will keep all of you posted."

Marckolius exits the bridge with Viktorlo. The elevator stops with Viktorlo exiting first. They walk through the unfinished areas until they reach a partially completed area.

"You're really going to ask them?"

"They're almost here," Marckolius puts his finger over his lips. "Commander Bruno and Lt. Commander Troas, please come in." Two vampires wearing army fatigues enter the room. Both of their images blow away like grains of sand in a heavy wind. "I wanted to talk to you since you are technically the leaders of those who escaped Desespero."

Commander Bruno steps forward, "Sir, it is an honor. We do have a request. We would like to go home when this is done."

Marckolius puts the white metal boots with high knee guards on, "Home?"

"Desespero"

Marckolius and Viktorlo look at each other briefly, "I'm sorry but the families that run the Proprietorship have thoroughly entrenched themselves into the Syndicate. We would have to overthrow them just so you could go home. You are both former military. You have to be strategizing how this could be done."

"I see your point but I had to ask."

"I understand. You do have options. You don't have to leave when this is done. You can stay with us," Marckolius puts his hand out to the Commander.

The Commander takes his hand tightly, "We will consider it, Sir."

"Good. On to what you are here for, Viktorlo will lead the group to take engineering. I will lead the group to take the bridge. I alone will be the one to confront my uncle. No one else is to confront him."

Viktorlo chimes in, "Part of us ramming and grappling the ship will be K.S. taking over the systems. They are not going to expect us to do this, let alone our advanced capabilities"

"We are looking forward to our revenge," the Commander states.

"And we are eager to provide that to you. Finish your prep; we arrive in a couple of hours." Marckolius puts on his malleable white leather overcoat.

The Commander and Lt Commander bow slightly, turn and return to their men.

Marckolius and Viktorlo return to the bridge. The wait continues until they prepare to exit Interdimensional Space. A countdown appears at the top of the front view screen in large white numbers.

"Preparing to exit ID Space," echoes throughout the ship.

"Exit coordinates are confirmed." One of the helmsmen announces.

Marckolius taps several keys on the command chair. A panel slides open to show an embedded bright gold ring. "This is what we salvaged from the briefcase you brought back from Propri."

"Then that was part of the scepter belonging to the Key?" Viktorlo looks closely at the embedded gold ring.

"Sir," One of the bridge officers start, "The enemy fleet is comprised of 150 ships. They are currently bombarding the planet. All life will be extinguished within the next minute."

"Let's hope that black box works Ophion." Marckolius looks at the countdown. "Charge all weapons and the central cannons. Put full power to the shields."

The exit vortex forms in front of them, swirling blue and white.

"Exiting ID Space in five, four, ready, steady, exiting . . ."

The entire fleet appears in the blink of an eye behind the Proprietor's fleet.

"Sir, the enemy fleet has yet to start planetary bombardment." One of the excited deck officers proclaim.

Marckolius pulls out his blue crystal. Ophion's eyes widen at the site. "You have the Key!"

"Prepare to broadcast the master key to the entire Proprietor fleet Kismet." Marckolius places the blue crystal into the bright gold ring on his chair. The center of the crystal lights up.

"Broadcasting the master key with full shut down commands," Kismet states.

Throughout the enemy fleet, ship after ship goes dark. "Fire all weapons. Destroy as many of them as possible before they reboot their ships!" Marckolius commands.

All forty ships launch mix colored orange-yellow balls of energy from their primary cannons. Missiles and laser turrets repeatedly fire. Blasts from the Remosian planetary cannons fire into the enemy fleet as well. Enemy ship after enemy ship explodes scattering debris throughout the area.

"Keep firing! Take down as many of the ships as possible." Marckolius stands with his hand clenched. He pulls the crystal from his command chair. The panel immediately closes up. "It's time for us to go Viktorlo. Brianto, you are in charge. Give us enough time to get in position and then ram the Cerci."

"They are down to 92 ships and counting, many of them are heavily damaged," Brianto sits in the command chair. "Order the fleet to clear the path to the Cerci. Since its back up we need to bring down her shields."

It takes several minutes for Marckolius and Viktorlo to reach the front wedge section of the ship. They take their positions with the rest of the men. The vibrations and sounds of the ship are very loud.

"We are in position." Viktorlo yells into the intercom.

"We are about to accelerate. The path is clear. We will be firing one last volley to bring down its shields. You're going to feel it!" Brianto answers from the bridge. A large rumbling noise erupts getting louder and louder before it dissipates. "Get ready, five, four, ready, steady, impact!"

Loud screeching of metal on metal reverberates through the ship. The shock of the impact knocks everyone off his or her feet. The sounds of six deafening explosions rumble through the wedge. Everyone falls to their knees with their hands over their ears.

"The grapplers are deployed. We have expanded our shields around the ship. K.S. is in the process of shutting down everything. Blow the doors and go!" Brianto's excited voice echoes through the wedge area of the ship.

"You heard him! Blow the doors and go!" Marckolius commands.

Multiple doors blow open. The boarding parties stream into the Cerci.

"Stay six meters from the men or they will get killed faster." Marckolius reminds Viktorlo as he slices into the approaching men, liquefying them as he goes. He stops long enough to turn to Viktorlo, "You go to the right to get to engineering. I'll go to the left."

Viktorlo nods. He and his men run down the metal gray corridor. A screeching noise echoes through the hall from the speakers, "This is K.S. I have turned off all weapons, propulsion, and have activated the internal dampening so no energy weapons can be fired. I have locked the elevators so only our men can use them. Happy hunting!"

The vampires swarm ahead clearing the path for Marckolius. Streaks of blood stretch into odd places and corridors. Screams of terror echo through the ship. Blood soaked corpses litter the deck.

'They've been busy.' Marckolius hears in his mind.

"Aren't you supposed to collect the souls of the dead?"

'Only the ones you dispatch. There are plenty of others that will eventually get around to collecting those souls.'

"Then people wonder why we have so many haunted places." Marckolius swings his sword cutting down two men, leaving behind blood soaked clothing in pools of blood. "There, you have something to do."

'Oh joy!'

Marckolius catches up to his men near the four central elevators. The two center sets of doors open.

"I am only going to need six men with me. Take the second elevator. I will go up alone in this one. The rest of you stand guard."

A resounding, "Yes Sir!" is heard from the men.

Marckolius exits first onto the bridge. The large windows show the destruction of his uncle's fleet. Debris fills the area with ship after ship that has survived with fires burning. The second elevator opens. The six vampires exit. Marckolius looks straight ahead and sees his uncle in his black uniform arguing with the Admiral.

"You fool, I told you to fire!" Duke Yoritus slams his hand down on the panel's large red button. The entire ship feels the jolt. A single missile is seen entering the Remosian atmosphere. The streak of the missile ends with a large explosion on the surface.

"Hello, UNCLE!" Marckolius announces his arrival. "You seem out of sorts."

"YOU!" the Duke yells. "You did this!" His eyes let off a bright red hue.

Marckolius steps forward near the command chair, staring at his uncle with a very bright red pulsing hue. "I have waited ten long years for this."

Marckolius' men subdue the last of the bridge crew and the Admiral. The Duke unclips his sword from his side and raises it across the command chair, almost touching Marckolius' sword. "Well nephew, you have caused me a lot trouble over these past ten years."

Marckolius lunges at him. Their swords spark on impact between each swing of the hardened metal. Sparks fly between them. The Duke swings and misses allowing Marckolius to side kick him in the ribs, pushing him back several meters. He moves, keeping the command chair between himself and Marckolius.

"Did you think this was going to be easy boy?"

"Answer me this uncle, why did you have my mother killed?"

"Still obsessing on that, huh? Well, she kept getting in the way of things and your pathetic father didn't have the guts to rich divorce her like he should have. As long as she lived we were at a disadvantage with the rest of the families."

"Really, and you thought that would help?"

"It should have allowed me to influence you. I did everything to strengthen our family's power and control. Whoever controls the money has the power."

The Duke lunges at Marckolius. Marckolius easily side steps him, blocking his attack. Their swords hit repeatedly causing many sparks. The Duke backs away again, "It's my turn to ask a question."

"Go ahead old man!"

"How did you manage to lower the shields and shutdown the weapons of my ships. And, how did you appear out of nowhere in the first place?"

"That's two questions. You only get one." Marckolius taunts with a smile. "I'll answer your first question. If you hadn't guessed it yet, I have the Key."

The Duke's eyes widen and his mouth opens slightly at the shock of the statement. Marckolius lunges at him, knocking him across the bridge into a far control panel.

"Impossible! The Key was lost."

"No, it was taken. My mother left it for me on Gregoria. I retrieved it shortly after her death!" Marckolius pauses for a moment. "Father was right; you are slow on the up take. I had the Key and used it over and over again, right under your nose."

"You bastard!" His uncle yells as he barely misses Marckolius. Their swords strike again. "Let me give you a lesson in blades boy. When we vibrate our blade and the blade hits bone small micro fractures occur. Over time this weakens your blade, even if you do have it resurfaced."

They pull apart, "So what?"

"My blade is new. Yours is very old. It's time to test its metal."

Duke Yoritus leaps at Marckolius. The blades spark after each hit and block. The blades move faster and faster until Marckolius' blade shatters. Shards fly in all directions. The Duke's sword cuts Marckolius on his left arm before he can leap away. He looks at what is left of his sword. The blade is nothing more than a longer than normal dagger with only one sharp side. The blade has shattered down to the hilt.

His uncle lets out a deep laugh, "You see boy, you will never take me down!"

He lunges after Marckolius, barely missing him. He continues slowly until he lunges at him again. Marckolius blocks the sword with his left arm, spinning into his uncle. Their eyes meet. Their noses come within millimeters of each other. What is left of Marckolius' sword twists up and through his uncle's ribcage. The small point of the blade protrudes through his uncle's back allowing small drops of blood to stain the back of his clothes.

His uncle drops his sword, falling to his knees before Marckolius. Marckolius looks down at him with deep resentment and anger. He takes a deep breath before kneeling down and picking up his uncle's sword. He looks at his uncle struggling in a feeble attempt to pull the shattered sword from his chest. Blood pours from the wound, dripping onto the floor in globs and staining his uncle's cloths.

"Any last words you evil Son of a Bitch?" Marckolius stares down at his uncle.

"If you kill me your father is dead! The other families will take him down. The contracts will become active and assassins from all over will attempt to collect the bounty. Your father and half-brothers will die horrid, painful deaths!"

"I had a chat with my father many months ago when I went to Propri and collected my mother's body. You know, so she could have the burial you prevented from happening." Marckolius reaches down and twists the sword in his uncle's chest. Duke Yoritus lets out a loud yelp of pain. "My father has taken precautions. After I'm done those fools will do everything they can to keep him alive!"

Marckolius raises his uncle's sword. His uncle puts his hands up, "Please, please don't. I am sorry. I'm sorry for everything. I was only doing what was best for our family."

Marckolius pauses, "Asking for mercy? You are asking the wrong person. It would be better for you to ask God because you are about to meet Him!" Marckolius swings his uncle's sword taking his uncle's head clean off. He stares down at his uncle's severed head taking several deep breaths, "At long last, it is done!"

CHAPTER 17

WELCOME TO
THE EMPIRE

MARCKOLIUS LOOKS OUT FROM THE observation deck of his command chip. A deep feeling of remorse overcomes him. He bows his head in silent prayer only to find himself standing above the remnants of the battle. He looks down to see the destroyed capital of Remos. Large chunks of his uncle's fleet float past him. Uniformed bodies float within the debris.

"All this and for what?" Marckolius wipes tears from his eyes. "All the souls lost because of my thirst for revenge? The relief that this is finally over and my mother's death is avenged cannot be the end of this."

'It's not over.'

"You really did it!" Marckolius spins around to see Princess Zorina staring at him. Her wondrous glittering red gown accentuates her glistening skin and green eyes.

"You look well. I take it you are fully healed?"

"I wanted to thank you for saving my life." She kisses him on the cheek. Sparks occur as their auras merge for a brief movement. "You must come to Elkri to receive a proper thank you. You will come?"

Marckolius places his hand on the spot she kissed, giving her a long look of surprise. "We should not be able to touch here."

"Then obviously there is more connecting us to each other than just your blood." She turns, walking away from him, "Be sure to come to Elkri after you are done cleaning up this mess."

"I will come once I figure out what I am doing next."

"It'll come to you. Destiny has a funny way of sneaking up on all of us," Princess Zorina fades away.

Marckolius opens his eyes to see the wide field of destruction from the observation deck.

'It had to be done!' He hears in his mind.

"I know. He had to be stopped, so much lost in so little time. So many lives destroyed. So many souls lost. All I ask is forgiveness from God."

'It is time. Someone must standup and lead.'

"I have to do this after all. I have to fill the void."

'Everyone has a calling. This is yours.'

Marckolius speaks with Viktorlo before entering the bridge to the cheers of everyone. "Damage report Brianto."

"Six ships with minor damage. Twenty-one crewmembers were injured, all on the six damaged ships. Out of the fifty boarding party members only three were lost and fourteen were injured but healing quickly."

"That is great news. The fleet is intact and now fully battle tested. It's time we go down to the surface."

Brianto walks over to him, "Marckolius, that shot from the Cerci took out the palace and the bunker beneath it. The royal family is dead. The government is gone."

"How, I thought K.S. deactivated all of the weapons systems on the Cerci?"

K.S. answers, "That particular system was of unknown technology. I figured out how to deactivate the rest of the missiles though."

"What about the loss of the Remosian government? And, what about your arm?" Brianto grabs Marckolius' left arm to try to look at the wound.

Marckolius pulls his arm away. "I'm fine. We are going to have to fill the power vacuum." Ophion and Brianto both look at Marckolius with surprise. "Viktorlo is getting the shuttle ready. We need to make a statement and I thought it would be best to do it from the surface."

Brianto, Telibina, and Ophion all follow Marckolius down to the hanger bay. They meet Viktorlo and board a shuttle down to the surface.

"Ophion, the unknown missile technology, was it Kaosian?" Marckolius asks.

Ophion looks down briefly, "Yes."

They fly over the blast crater surveying the destruction. Their shuttle lands in the courtyard of what was the palace. When they exit, many older men greet them. They bow when Marckolius exits the shuttle.

"We are humbled by your presence," the Chief Elder states as he holds out a very old looking book. "Please accept this as our gratitude for saving our planet."

Marckolius walks up to them; taking the book he opens it. "I see you are the Elders, the keepers of the Remosian history and that of Earth." He thumbs through the book. After several minutes, Marckolius closes the book and hands it back to the Chief Elder. "This is far too precious for me to accept."

"This is a copy of our history and journey to Remos. Is this not a worthy enough gift?" Concern spreads across their faces.

"You misunderstand." He moves closer to the Chief Elder, "We're not leaving."

The Elders concern is replaced with joy as Marckolius walks out to the center of the courtyard. Viktorlo plants a pike before him, and then moves to his right. Brianto holds out an open black box.

"Begin the transmission to the Proprietorship and the known worlds within our sphere."

The Communications Officer sets the camera on its tripod. The red light turns on, "This is K.S. The broadcast is going through the communications grid on Propri right now. They are attempting to block it. No further issues, ready . . ."

"Most of you know me but for those of you who don't, I am Marckolius Taranus Anglicus. I stand here today on Remos. Those still wondering or have not yet heard, the Proprietors' glorious armada has been defeated. As proof I present Duke Yoritus' head." He turns, pulls the Duke's head from the box, and places it on the pike. The Duke's eyes are wide open. Marckolius pushes down on the head until it is firmly in place. Blood drips from the severed neck.

"Now then, I will make you a promise. As long as my father continues to be King of the Proprietorship, you need not worry about me coming and doing the same to each of the ruling families. Given this promise, I sure do hope you arrange to protect my father and half-brothers. For your sake I hope he has a long healthy life." Marckolius smiles broadly.

"So, what's next? Let me explain in simple terms. We are building a new government here. Remos will be the capital. Each planet within our sphere, and as we expand, will be given a choice to join us or not. For those that join us, you will fall under our protection. You will still govern yourselves but through the implementation of a representative democracy. Each member planet will elect a primary and alternate representative to what will be the Royal Council." Marckolius smiles again.

"Oh yes, what will we call this new government, this new protectorate per say?" After a short pause, his crystal blue eyes glow with a red hue, "Welcome to the Empire, the Remosian Empire!"